The Anunnaki Project

By Aaron J Weaver

Part One

The Anunnaki Project

Prologue

Some call them the Reptilians. It is more respectful to call them the Saurians. They are the progeny of the dinosaurs. Certain of their members have instructed the author. They have shared the following record of events. The author has been tasked to give an explanation of the origin of the human species. Then the greater task is to explain our current dilemma. The greater task is to warn humanity.

Humanity is a created species. The complete tale has never been told. Our tale began with a few Anunnaki, driven by desperate necessity. Only tattered pieces of the story have survived our calamitous history.

We face a present disaster, a hidden disaster. We must expand our understanding. Our species now faces an unseen challenge. The Huns are at the gate. We are not prepared. Most of us are not even aware.

There exist countless species in our galaxy. They hail from innumerable solar systems. They traverse the space-ways. They travel to twice the speed of light.

We do not understand their societies. But all life comes from a common set of patterns. They trade, they politic, they teach and learn, they deceive, they dominate.

Humanity arrived late to the galactic scene. We are by no means the first species to grace the galaxy. We are the second on this Earth. We are the third in this solar system.

The Anunnaki where the first. They originated on a large moon of Saturn. That moon has since subsided under Saturn's atmosphere. It still orbits under Satern's surface. They still occupy it.

The second species originated on this Earth. They precede humanity by many millennia. They are not mammals. They are the progeny of the dinosaur. We are little aware of their existence.

Now, eight foreign species operate on this planet. They are new arrivals. No one invited them. They are all Huns at the gate. They work against our best interests.

We must learn the nature of inter-species relations. We must understand exo-politics. A very unfortunate future awaits an ignorant species.

Our fate affects the Saurians. Therefore our elder siblings have provided this teaching. We must understand our beginning. From there we can forge an understanding of our adversaries.

This is the story of our beginning. We are the creation of the first species of this solar system. We are a product of the Anunnaki.

What follows is the communications between the Anunnaki which created us. This is an explanation of how and why they fashioned the human race.

DESIGN OF ROTHA

To Kin

Congratulations on your creation of the abomination. Your deed has reached every waking ear. I am greatly relieved that our great King has sanctioned your creation. Even the Chief of Priests has made exception for your creation. Your bold gamble bore fruit. Now all waking eyes are upon us.

Now tell me the status of your testing program. How does the abomination respond to our orders?

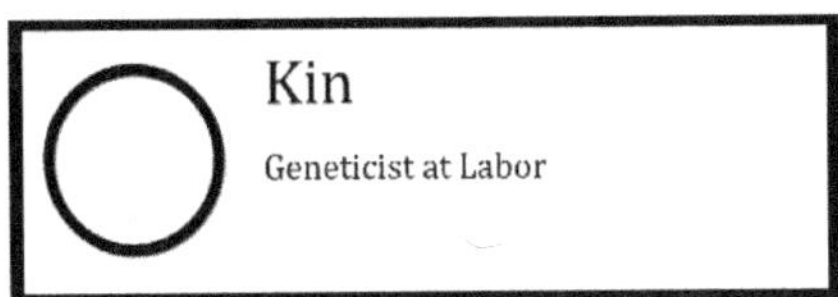

To Baron Rotha

The abomination can understand our commands and use our tools. That much is a success. But they are not controllable as a workforce. My initial tests have all been failures. This initial prototype is not suited for our present task.

I remind myself that this is only the first prototype. I expect many trials before a suitable worker can be created.

With so many possible paths to explore, I feel an uncertainty of how best to proceed.

See attached Lab Notes

Kin, Lab notes, Personal Log, Earth year plus 125

I failed a dozen times. I wasted the lives of a dozen priests. After so many failures I pricked myself. I hastily drew my own flesh and blood. After ten minutes I had isolated my DNA and morpho-genetic fluid.

I thought little of my actions. I admit I acted out of desperation. But my actions seemed to flow without effort or deliberation. In three days I had achieved a viable lifeform. It could live while sustained in an artificial womb.

Perhaps my technique had been perfected over the course of a thousand such operations. But it seemed the result was too easy. The process went without flaw. That almost never happens. Usually it is a struggle not a flow.

In twenty days I had an accelerated development fetus. I observed the prototype had a peculiar appearance. It looked very different from the fetus of my other experiments.

In thirty-eight days I had an independent life-form. I took samples for future experimentation and destroyed the life-form. At that point I realized I had broken the law. I remembered the law and ethics of the Anunnaki. I realized I had created an abomination. I remembered that the law forbids the mixing of Anunnaki genes with any genetic creation. I contemplated that my life might be forfeit for producing an abomination.

I contemplated requesting a variance to the law. Instead, I proceeded with my experiments.

I produced a full batch of abominations. I was still uncertain if they could be raised to age.

They looked very different from other primates. Their teeth are not carnivorous. Their eyesight is not good at night. They have fairly large brains. They have a hair pattern reverse of primates. They have hair on their heads. But their bodies are mostly bald. They have a distinct nose which protrudes. They are very unlike the hairy man of the forest.

They showed promise from the very first. My tests showed they have good natural language potential. They have a very agile hand. They can use any tool which they can lift.

I kept them quarantined in the small lab for twenty years. I observed their natural behavior. Then I destroyed them.

I pondered over this experiment for three more years. When Rotha called for a progress report I confessed to my deeds. The previous 120 years had been a string of abysmal failures. Now I had produced a viable candidate.

I had only added 0.33% of my DNA. The effect of my morphogenetic fluids was likely a greater contributor. This small genetic modification gave me the first hope of success. I confessed to Rotha. Rotha gave no communication for three months. During this time I feared for my life.

Rotha returned with a variance to the law. My heart blossomed like the sunrise. He made an unending speech about the gravity of our situation. He made it clear that the variance was a historic. It was an unprecedented exception to the law.

The abomination has been approved. Now I can get to work.

To Kin

Standby, I will create an official order to give further direction and clarity to our project.

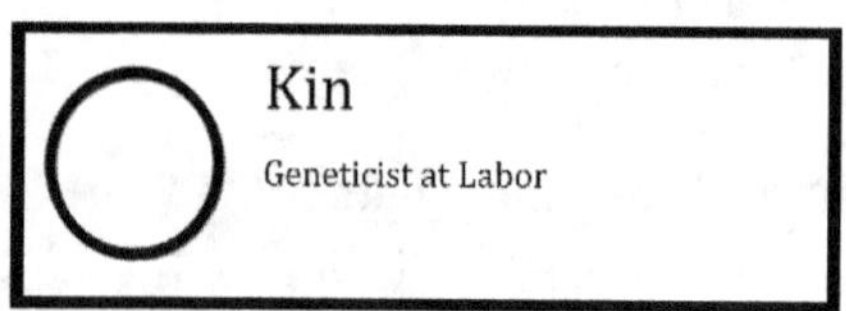

To Baron Rotha

As I standby, I have birthed a second prototype of the abomination. I expected a greater change. This second prototype is genetically quite different but behaves largely the same.

Lab Notes Attached

Kin, Lab notes, Personal Log, year plus 151

I continue to be impressed by the size and strength of the abomination. They are seven times my height. They would crush me with one step. They are nearly as tall as the Igigi. They have four times more physical strength than the Igigi. As with all mammals, the males have physical conflict to determine hierarchy. When they fight It fills my heart with terror.

Their stench fills my nose. I have abandoned the small lab. My Igigi created a larger facility.

After I export them from the birthing lab they spend the rest of their days in the new facility. The Igigi are large, the Igigi have no sense of smell. Therefore only the Igigi deal directly with the abomination.

To Kin

An official decree from the Office of Baron Rotha,

Lord of Anunnaki Genetic Programs

To Kin, Geneticist at Labor

As you have successfully created the abomination. As it can use our tools and understand our orders. But it is not controllable to labor in the mines.

Hear my decree.

As we have been awakened from cyber-sleep,

As a royal order has selected us for a tour of wake-full duty,

That this duty may endure up to one thousand Earth years,

Accepting that our only duty is to the King and the greatness of the Anunnaki people:

Therefore, hear my command.

It is my will that the abomination be controllable.

It is my will, that I give the commands of what they will and will not perform.

Therefore, design for me, woven into the very fabric of their flesh, impressed into the very nature of their minds – that they will reliably perform and not perform at my command.

That they will not command themselves or each other, so that they may not escape or usurp my command.

Hear my order, so signed this day,

Baron Rotha

Lord of Anunnaki Genetic Programs

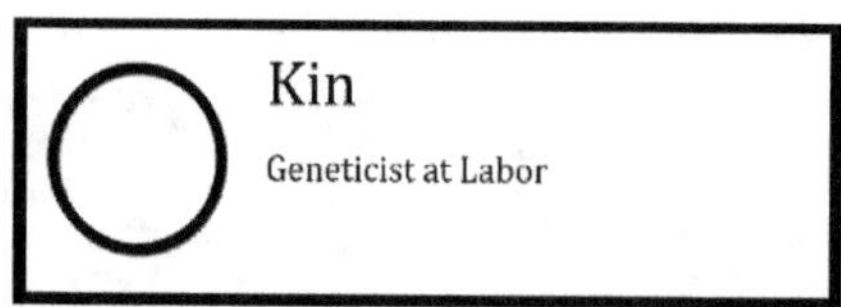

To Baron Rotha

From the hand of Kin Geneticist at labor.

I accept that I have been commanded awake. I accept that I have been torn from the sweet worlds of cyber-sleep. I accept the exceptionally long term of this project. I realize the vital importance of this project. I will give all my skill and attention to this project. I am yours to command.

To the success of your order, I consent and give all.

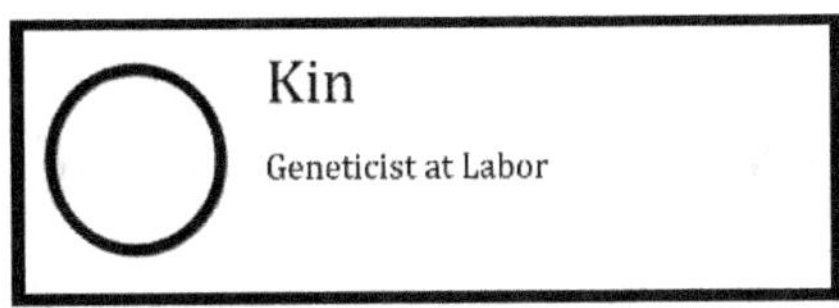

To Baron Rotha

I recall the saying, better a beggar in cyber-sleep than a king awake. But enough complaining, let's talk task. I received your order. I set to planning immediately.

The dynamic I face is very demanding. Simple creatures are easy to control. The abomination we design must perform complex tasks.

Our calculations are conclusive. Machines cannot accomplish our task in time. Since the Igigi revolted they are no longer an option. Our people will not travel to the Earth to mine gold. Therefore the abomination is a last and desperate option.

I am designing them for complex tasks. We cannot command them at each individual task. They must grow their own food. They must build their own housing. They must raise the next generation of abomination. Our remaining loyal Igigi are few. The abomination must have leadership from their own ranks.

I do not know of any control mechanism to accomplish your command. I do not have any genetic patterns in my library to complete your order. But I remain hopeful and committed to your order. I remain committed to the success of our project.

Any further clarification of the nature of the task will be appreciated.

To Kin

The task before us is greatly difficult. I commend you for your dedication. You are breaking new ground. Your name will be honored in our history when we succeed.

This will be the first solar nova that does not utterly ravage our planet. This will be the first nova that does not set our planet's progress back thousands of years. We will be the first to avoid the wrath of a nova.

This time we will maintain our delight within cyber-sleep. We will not be forced to swarm the planet's surface. We will not be required to wake from the vaults to rebuild. Our lives will not be shortened out of our vaults. We will not suffer the strain, stress and danger of laboring to rebuild. This is even more important now that the Igigi have abandoned us.

Following the patterns of nature, I foresee two types of abomination. One type will lead and the other will perform the work. The leaders must be supremely obedient to our command. The leaders must be more simple-minded. The leaders must be steady in focus. They need only comprehend our command and understand that it is performed.

The worker must have a more intelligent mind. The worker must have a faster and more flexible mind, so it can figure out how to accomplish the task. The workers must be incomplete so they will cling to the leaders. The workers must be strong and full of energy. But they must be timid in heart and soul, so they will cling to the leaders.

All the abomination must lack a key which we hold. All abomination must have a lack which they seek to fill. All abomination must turn to us to fulfill an unfillable need.

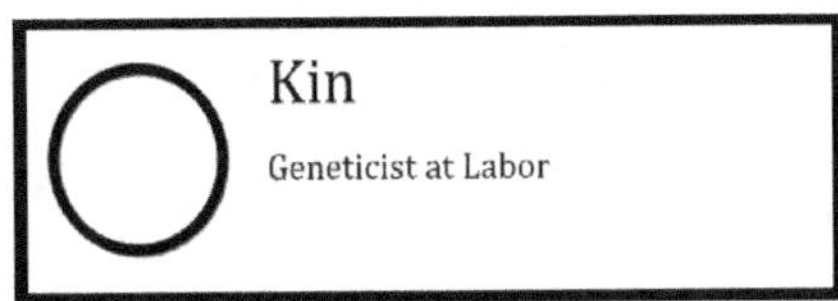

To Baron Rotha

I see the wisdom of two sub-species of abomination. I have begun preliminary work toward your vision. I have created a program to model gene expression. I work toward the two types of abomination. I will use this as a specification for all future creations.

I have not made progress toward a key which only we hold.

To Kin

I envision a hunger of the mind and heart. I feel there is a longing that dwells in all sentient beings. I envision it can be used as motivation.

The abomination will turn to us like a child turns to its mother. The abomination will wait on us to fill its need. We will fill their hearts with inspiration. Our command to work will be the key which causes their passion to flow.

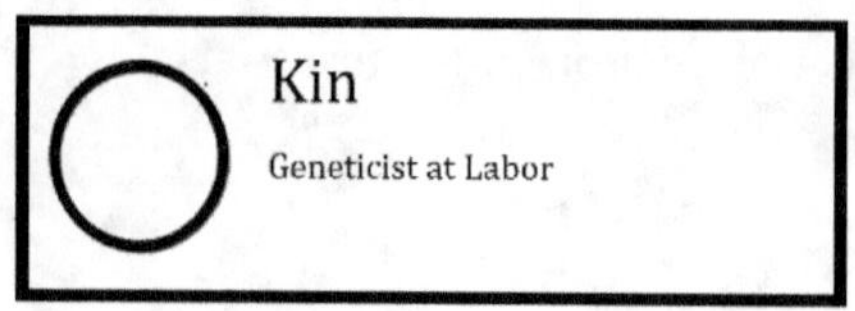

To Baron Rotha

I fear they will turn to each other to fill the need. They must have leadership from their own ranks. I fear they may usurp our command. What can we use to inspire and lead them?

Lab notes attached.

Kin, Lab notes, year plus 278

I allowed them to reproduce to a population of fifty-five abomination. I deem this to be the maximum capacity of the facility. At a population of thirty they self-divided into two groups. At full capacity they have divided into three groups.

I observe considerable friendship and even interbreeding between groups. Even so, each individual knows to which group they belong. When a fight erupts everyone knows if it is within the group or between groups. Individuals nearly always side with their group. Only rare and particularly intelligent individuals have been known to choose friendship over group loyalty.

The abomination are capable workers when directly overseen. Without direct oversight they invariably fail. I have not yet conceived of a way to control them without constant direct management. I believe their mammalian pack hierarchy is the key to control them.

To Kin

I reason out the problem thus, all sentient beings understand their own good and best interest. All sentient beings have access to truth through intuition and imagination. All sentient beings have direct access to the source. All higher beings intuitively know their best interest.

No one can withhold this from a sentient being.

Now we confront the real challenge. How then do we make a being which is incomplete? How do we make a being which is not aware of its own best interest? Only some form of incompleteness will bind them to our will.

I reason that intuition and imagination are the adversary.

Can you create a physical response to imagination within the abomination? Can you cause imagination to stir up so much energy as to panic or overwhelm? Then the truth born of imagination will then be nullified and defeated.

I am a generator of ideas. I give feedback to your ideas. Together we must push into unknown territory. We must create a new architype of life. This is the only way we can complete this most urgent project.

We have only eight hundred and fifty-seven Earth years until this project must reach completion.

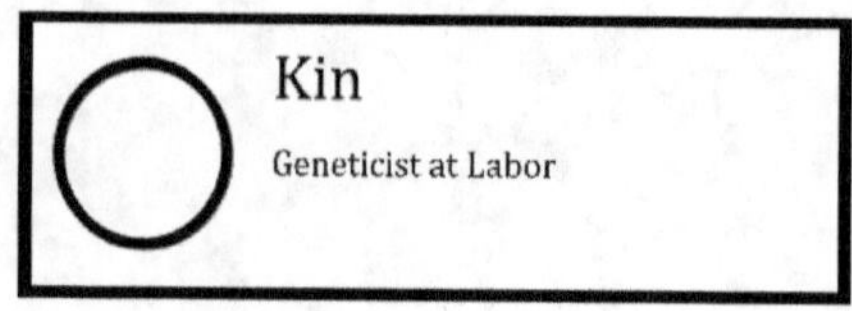

To Baron Rotha

Your words inspire me. I honor your cunning.

I see suppressing imagination and intuition as a central aim. Every sentient being contains the whole of the All-man. No one has ever brought life to a sentient being which lacks the All-man. So the abomination will understand its essential purpose and best interest.

Neuro-genetics only has three tools. I can enliven, depress or confuse. My three tools can intensify, diminish or mix-up stimuli paths.

Using these three tools I can act on your idea. I can make a response to imagination. When imagination occurs, it can cause an over-stimulating excitement. I will conduct further experimentation.

But I still lack a clear view of how this will become motivation. We are, after all, seeking to motivate and de-motivate. I need more perspective on the foundations of motivation.

To Kin

I have a contact which may be helpful. I will welcome him to the conversation. He is of high rank among our people. He is not of the Royal Family. Regard him with dignity and forbearance.

To Kin and Chief Priest Tar

Welcome Chief Priest Tar to the conversation, Tar, Chief Priest of the holy priests of all Anunnaki.

All hail the All-man. All hail the holy priests. Highest honors to their lifelong labor to understand the All-man. All hail the priests, who deny themselves the pleasures of cyber-sleep in order to study and meditate.

Our gratitude to the priests. Our gratitude to those who deny themselves the long life of cyber-sleep in order to keep their life-spark pure. May we remember our debt to the priests as we build worlds of wonder and delight in cyber-sleep.

I welcome most distinguished Chief Priest Tar to the conversation. I honor your cherished priests who give soul to our creations. I personally honor the sacrifice of each priest. I am humbled as they transfer their essence to each new prototype. Let their essence live on forevermore. I extend our welcome and our thanks.

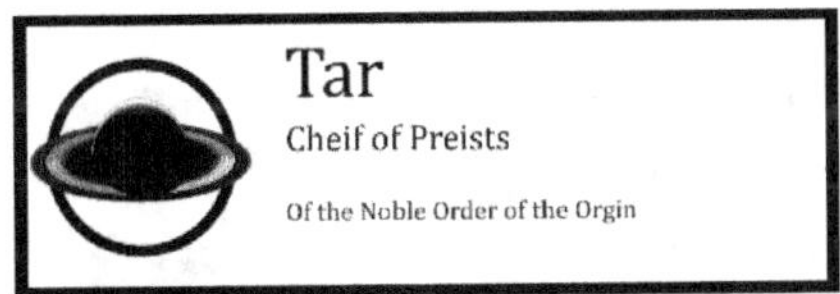

To Baron Rotha and Kin

I answer your call. I am of the All-man. I am with the All-man. May the All-man lighten our way.

I abhor cyber-sleep and the unnatural long life it gives. Remember us not in your realms of falsity.

Your inquiry denies me meditation and study. Nevertheless, because your project is vital to protect our planet, I consent.

As I have read, your conversation of late touches on motivation. I have an answer. As read in all common scriptures, the Origin-mind invades the physical realm to feed. The Origin-mind extends into the physical realm. It bifurcates and morphs as it pushes into the physical realm. Eventually the Origin-mind expresses as each living organism. As it is written, "we wear a dirt shirt, we each dance in a meat suit, the All-man clothed in the dust."

The Origin-mind invades the physical realm to feed. But what food does a mind need? What food does a spirit need to survive? The Origin-mind needs no physical food. Mind requires only attention. Mind requires new cognizance. The food of the Origin-mind is experience. And here we are at the answer. To *experience* is the foundational motivation of all life.

See attached scripture:

Let me know if I can further elucidate.

Common scripture: Words given to Hoth from the fifth density being Jerrototha. Chapter 5, Verse 3-8

Verse 3. Behold and understand, this shall you know and always remember, that nothing within your thoughts belongs to you. Nor can you own it. Nor can you keep it forever. But all thought comes from these three; the *mental domain*, the *pool of being* and the *Origin-mind*.

Verse 4. Firstly, behold the *mental domain*, A mental universe, an ocean of consciousness, the page upon which all thought and emotion is written. No mortal can hope to comprehend the mental domain. No mortal being can hope to comprehend its vastness.

Verse 5. Secondly , Within the mental domain are endless *pools of being*. Each pool of being is a sea in which the blobs of pure emotion reside. Our pool is but one of an uncountable number.

Within the pool reside an uncountable myriad of blobs. Each blob - indistinct yet individual. Each blob - a pure part of emotion. Each blob - a pure component of thought. Even our most simple experience is composed of many, many blobs.

The blobs are the nucleotides out of which the DNA of thought are composed. Each blob - the atom out of which complex emotions are formed. Each blob - a molecule out of which the body of thought and perception are composed. Each blob - a word with which is written the book of thought and emotion.

Verse 6. No being, in its normal state of awareness, can experience the pure emotions. No being in its normal state of awareness can know the pure components of thought. Only the adept sage can experience such a pure and singular realization. The experience of each blob is a gift which cannot be taken back to the living. Only a shadow of the realization can remain.

Verse 7. Thirdly, hail the *Origin-mind*. Like a worm among the flotsam, it is singular and supreme among the denizens of our pool of being. Hail the Origin-mind, king among the proto-blobs, most prominent of all the roots of consciousness. Hail the Origin-mind.

Verse 8. The Origin-mind attacks the crumb of the physical domain; its spindly emanations reach in to feed. The Origin-mind willfully invades. It injects itself into the crumb. It forces in its tendrils. They become each expression of life. The tendrils communicate between the pool of being and each individual mind.

The Origin-mind invades the physical, so that we may experience, and thereafter return that experience as food to the Origin-mind. Therefore, let us experience deeply, that we may fulfill our purpose.

Common scripture: The words of Samonter.

Chapter 165

Then on a bed of jasmine and mushrooms I slept awake. And continued the journey set afore. Beginning as before, with the wreathing and pure sensation - That of *the initiation of action*.

How else can it be described but as the *initiating of action*? I have since recognized that pure feeling so many times. That feeling is mixed into so many emotions. I feel it surge whenever a possibility may lead to action.

But in its pure form it overwhelms and burns. The burning of *Pure initiation* began my journey, once again into the vastness of the galaxy.

Setting aside the vision of the pool, setting aside the swamp of blobby impurities. I enjoined the Origin-mind. Such an experience cannot be told. The small individual mind cannot contain the great and vast mind. The teacup cannot hold the ocean. Only an individual mind, expanded by sham-la-poo, can go beyond its own boundaries. Only the mind of the adept can mix with that which is so vast.

There I felt a rush and a push, fierce as a wolfs growl, strong as a bull rushing in. The Origin-mind's first will is to enter and push. It pushes in and then flows in, as if through roots or tubes. The inrush has the feeling of a particular color - that of dazzling white and silver. The inrush is like the sound of sirens singing. It feels like the rumble of rock dragging and rolling below a roaring mountain river.

Every inrushing tentacle soon meets an impediment. Every impediment causes a divide. Every divide leads to a, as it were, fork in the road. A spider web of divides, a lattice work structure, but it does not therefore have an overall shape. Such a web of bifurcations is a mental construct. It is only my understanding of its function.

Each divide lets go of some certain attribute. Each divide splits the whole of the pool into smaller and more concise expressions. And yet each part of the whole contains all of the whole. The Origin-mind is present in all parts. But certain aspects are suppressed. Finally, the trail of inrushing ends. It ends with a face. Each face is the end of a long line of inrushing.

Now at the end of the line it begins the return journey. From each individual expression a line of return traces back. Each individual gains something in the physical domain. Each individual initiates a stream. The stream flows back to the Origin-mind.

These visions of the Origin-mind are beyond the understanding of any individual. We strive to understand. Of all the ideas we know, the one which fits best is *food*. The Origin-mind is feeding. The Origin-mind is like a mold invading a crumb. It pours itself into the crumb. It exudes something of itself. Then it takes back that which has been digested from the crumb.

The physical domain is that crumb. Only the Origin-mind takes the challenge to attack the physical domain. The blobs in the pool of being wait passively. The Origin-mind attacks the conspicuous crumb of physical reality.

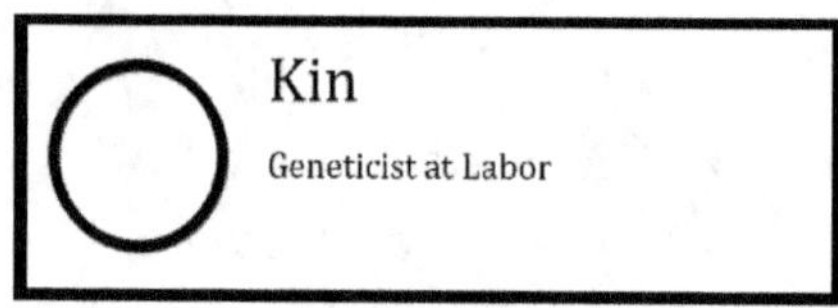

To Chief Priest Tar and Baron Rotha

I am familiar with the common scriptures. I find myself wanting further elucidation.

I understand the theory of the Origin-mind. I've seen the evidence for the Blue Avians. If they do exist, I wish they would give me access to their genetic library. I need a galaxy worth of genes to complete this baffling task.

If one of their city ships came by, I would gladly learn from them. If they do seed all planets with life, I am in a way their student.

The abomination have high potential. They are natural builders. I fear I have given them too much ability. I fear they may become a future threat to us.

I gave them a degree of vocal ability. I and the Igigi constructed a symbolic language for them. We denied them an objective or foundational language. We gave them a symbolic language based on nothing but arbitrary symbols. They speak with nothing but arbitrary sounds.

After all this I still have a wide question. How do I motivate the abomination? How do I command them without fail? What secret does the All-man hold that can guide our quest?

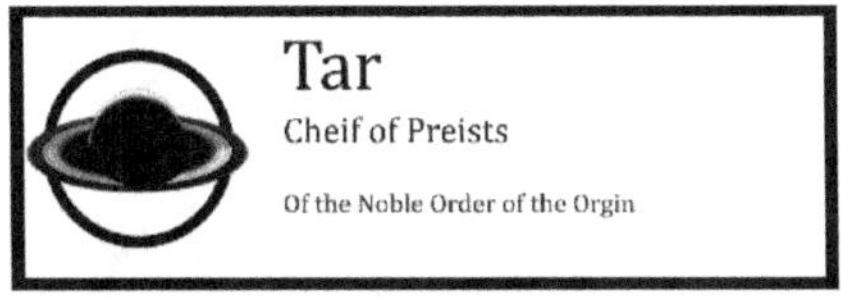

To Baron Rotha and Kin

Why am I bothered with questions only fit for a common researcher? The priests' study with the upmost discipline. There is no greater calling than the life of a priest. These are questions for a geneticist.

To Kin

(Reserved for your eyes only)

We welcome the valued perspective of the priests. Do not antagonize Chief Priest Tar. The dialogue has begun properly with fundamental subjects. We will proceed step by step until we discover the successful answer.

Do not bring the theories of the priests into doubtful question.

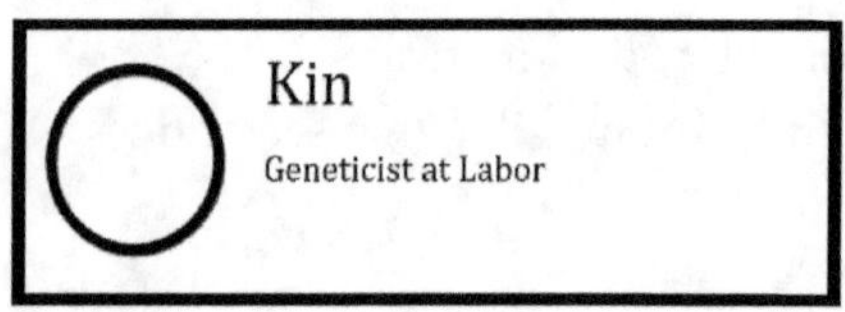

To Chief Priest Tar and Baron Rotha

With all due respect, I still call for assistance. Here is the path which has led to my current question.

I made another prototype in an attempt to fulfill Baron Rotha's new command.

I created a line of transfer-neurons from their pineal gland to their language centers. This way intuition will become language. Intuition becomes an understanding made of language. This way they will not learn intuition directly. They will only understand and communicate with language. Their language is oppressively primitive.

Another effect of this mechanism is that they can only receive from the pineal. They cannot transmit thoughts telepathically. Understandings received from the pineal translate to language. They have a primitive and unfounded language. It cannot translate back to a fundamental understanding. Their language cannot be communicated through the pineal. They are blocked from the most fundamental form of communication - telepathy. They cannot even understand the communications of animals. They certainly cannot command the animals.

I'm pleased with this cunning design, but it has a problem. The abomination daydream perpetually. A constant imagination fills their mind with word-based understandings. These understandings are mostly a confusion. Mostly they chase word associations. Their heaps of words bring them no closer to enlightenment.

I designed this mechanism to prevent imagination from enlightening them. Enlightenment would make them lazy. Under the cunning direction of Baron Rotha, I made the inflow of imagination overstimulating. The overstimulation interferes with the remembering of intuition. The overstimulation interferes with the memory retention of dreams and imaginations.

Unfortunately, it also interferes with keeping focus on one subject. It interferes with their general focus on work.

But even such a cunning design has not given success toward our new goal. The abomination are kept but not commanded.

I still lack clarity. How do we motivate the abomination? How do we ensure they obey only our command?

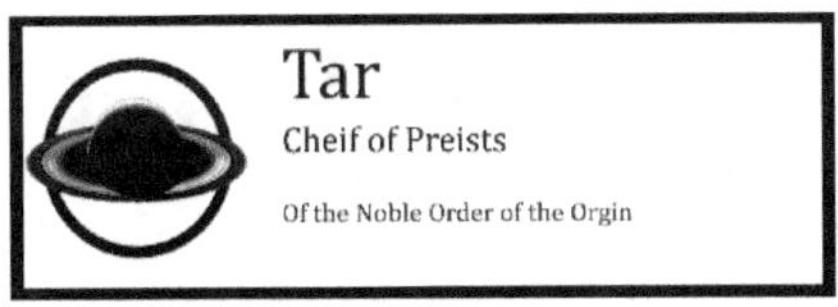

To Baron Rotha and Kin

The word abomination is fitting indeed. Am I to commit the precious life of any one of my priests to this project? Should such a gem as one of my own be sacrificed to give soul to these abominations? To create a creature so crippled, so confused, so oppressed, so far from the perfect whole of the All-man; the creature you created is indeed an abomination and a horror. If your cause was not so urgent to all Anunnaki I would refuse my help. I only help in order that you may not consume every one of my priests.

To Chief Priest Tar and Kin

I hail the priests and the wisdom of the scriptures. Oh Tar, I call on your assistance because we have no answer. I see your wisdom in laying the foundations of our conversation on common scripture. Our dialogue must be productive. So much depends on it.

We have created a prototype which can fulfill the original order. They can work all day, use our tools and understand our commands. I honor the priests so sacrificed who gave soul to these prototypes.

Now we face a greater problem, the problem of free will. I understand that the All-man contains free will. I know this can not be denied. The Igigi also have free will. They abandoned us in our hour of greatest need.

We must be clever. We must depress the abominations energy until we call for it. Then our command must inspire them.

Our technology is not capable of infringing on their free will. But they must obey when my command fills them with energy. Tell me if you see truth in my design.

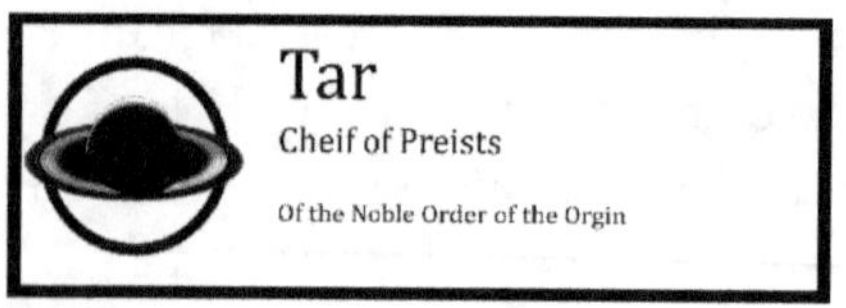

To Baron Rotha and Kin

Do you think I fail to understand your quest? Do you imagine that I do not personally know and love every priest which I have sent? You must understand that I am greatly unsettled by this project.

Now ask yourself, what if *I* were the abomination? The fundamental teaching of all scriptures is that we are all one. We are all an expression of the Origin-mind. We are all the All-man. The All-man is not somewhere else. It is not abstract or far away. It is I. I am the All-man.

If we are each the All-man, then ask yourself, if I were the abomination –
what then? If it were you – what then?

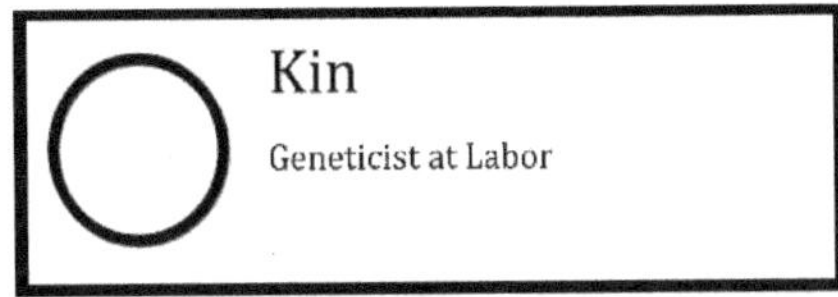

To Chief Priest Tar and Baron Rotha

I also heed the scriptures and honor the sacrifice of every priest. I have
watched each one. I have been present as each priest sacrifices themself at
the foot of the abomination to be. I cried for the young priest who
ensouled our latest prototype. I wish they did not have to die to transfer
their spark.

This latest prototype had become my best hope. But this abomination is
un-controllable.

I had such hope in this prototype. But after three generations I see this
abomination will not serve us. I fear they will not complete the tasks
ordered. I fear they will go their own way the moment they are away from
their task master. I feel hope slipping away. I fear the failure of our project.

To Kin and Chief Priest Tar

Our task is absolutely vital. My command stands.

It is my will that the abomination obey my command. That I shall command what they will and will not do. They must reliably perform or withhold performance on command.

It will be wired into the fabric of their nature.

They must be in a ready, but in a de-energized state, until commanded. They must lack the key to self-motivation. I must be the spark that lights their fire of activity.

They must be lazy and unfocused without my key.

This is my urgent command. It stands now.

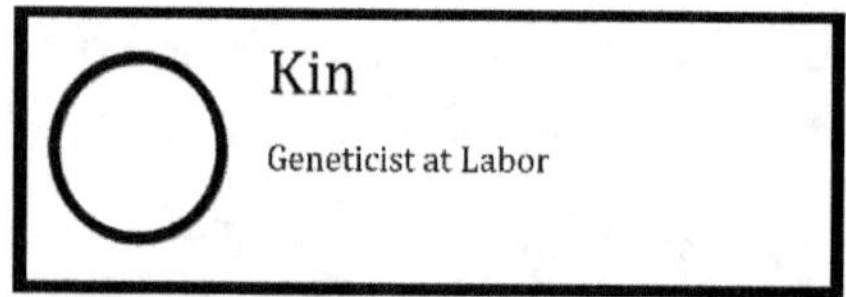

To Baron Rotha and Chief Priest Tar

I must report a failure. I designed my latest prototype to fulfill your order. I always base the new prototype on the last. I make many improvements which each new prototype. I only erase what is specifically malfunctioning. All the additions of every old type add into each new prototype.

They were supposed to become excited when complex commands stimulate the frontal cortex. Complex commands did stimulate a fire of energy and attention. Complex commands relieved them of a lazy stupor. I believed only we could give commands complex enough to stimulate them.

It appeared to work at first. Then they learned to tell each other stories. They concocted ridiculous and complex stories. The stories were not true or correct. But they did stimulate the listeners.

The best storytellers became the center of attention. Next the strongest alphas made alliance with the best storytellers. The story tellers would enliven the people. Then the alphas would give orders.

Soon the troop became excessively loyal to the alphas. They hesitated to obey my direct commands. They waited for the alpha and his storyteller to approve before they would obey. I destroyed this prototype.

I always keep a remnant of every prototype. They are saved alive in stasis. They may prove useful for future experimentation. This new genetic mechanism might prove useful as a future motivational sub-structure. But in their current form they are a failure.

To Kin and Chief Priest Tar

Congratulations on a partially successful design. The results did not meet my order. But the experience gained is worth every effort.

Let us plan carefully. We wish to minimize the priests so spent.

List what factors reduce excitement. By what neural pathways is excitement inspired?

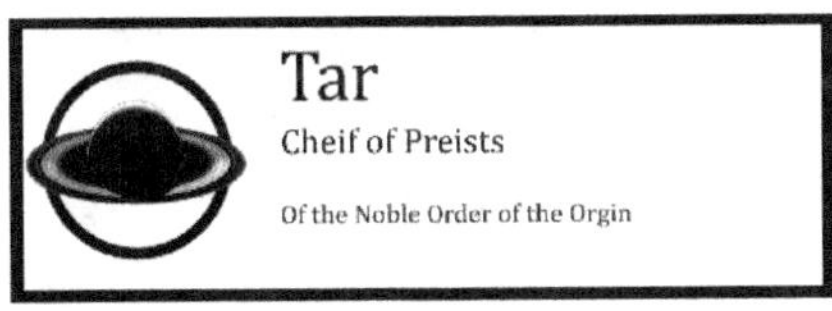

To Baron Rotha and Kin

Enough! Think secondly of neural path. Think first of intent. Think first of the heart behind the intent.

Think secondly of biological factors and genetics. Think first of relationship. Think first of friendship and alliance. Think first of personal contact and social bonds.

"Love the All-man first. We are all the All-man, everything else follows."

Walk the path with love, not lusting for results, not seeking victory for any self. Instead let every success glorify the All-man.

This is the way for all, even the abomination.

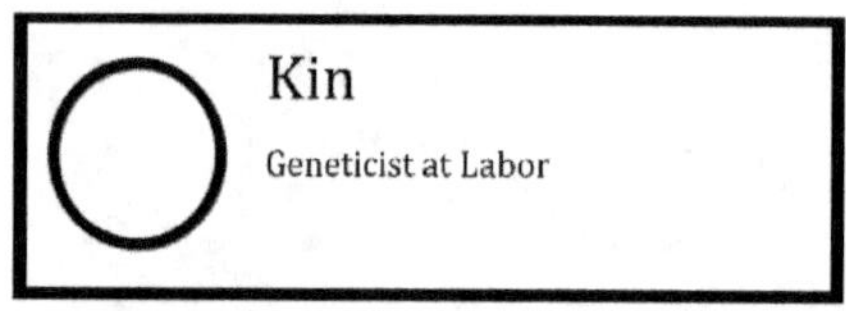

To Baron Rotha

(Reserved for your eyes only)

Tar's admonitions sparked an idea. I tell you in private because it is the opposite of his intent.

All my efforts have focused on individual motivations. I have not considered motivation within the group.

I have observed a strong bond of love within every group of abomination. They bond strongly to the tribe. The tribe is family.

I believe I can interrupt their familial love. If their love is interrupted, then our command may be made to restore that love. This may be the key we seek.

The current prototype daydreams perpetually. I believe I can cause their imagination to stimulate love. It is a simple matter to create pathways to link the pineal to both the language and love centers.

Their perpetual imagination will lead to perpetual love. They will have happy imaginations all day. This will fatigue the love production centers. The result will be desensitization. Perpetual use will fatigue the love response.

I believe I can cause some aspect of our command to interrupt their daydreams. What makes this all possible is that the love response recharges very quickly. Our command will interrupt the lovely daydream. Then the love capacity will replenish. The result will be a flood of love when our command is finished. This will associate love with our command.

This is only a conceptual hypothesis.

To Kin

(Reserved for your eyes only)

You are wise to address me personally on this issue. We wish to avoid antagonizing one we rely on absolutely. I have hesitations concerning your idea.

The honored Tar might quote common scripture, "Love is the currency of the All-man. Love is the spice that feeds the Origin-mind."

We must be delicate as we work with fundamental emotions such as love. I am not banning the principle. I advise extreme caution. Communicate such ideas to me alone.

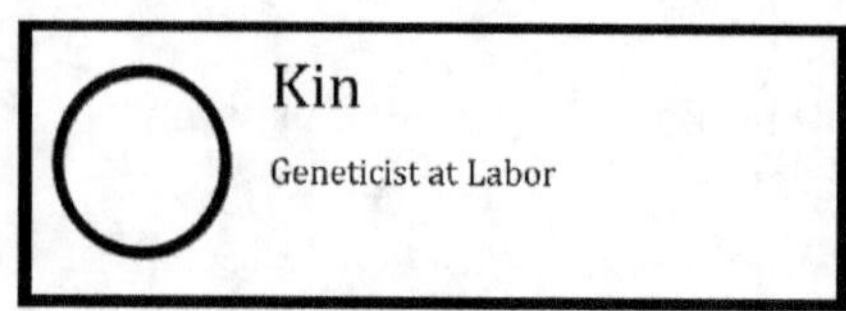

To Baron Rotha

(Reserved for your eyes only)

On the subject of love, there are only three possibilities. We can interrupt, stimulate or confuse. Those are my only options. A geneticist only has few fundamental tools.

Every function in biology can be described as a frequency, a frequency of how often it functions. Every neuron must fire. Every muscle must contract. Every cell must divide. It is only a question of how often. How often is the frequency.

All biological functions contain base frequencies. A neuron has a resting frequency of firing. A neuron will fire spontaneously at its base frequency unless it is stimulated or interrupted.

A cell will divide in a certain time unless accelerated or retarded. The technology of cyber-sleep aims to slow cell division to a minimum. That is how it provides a life span of hundreds of thousands of years.

We must account for all of nature's default frequencies. I need a better understanding of the actual labor the abomination will perform. Then I can modify the base frequencies to the work.

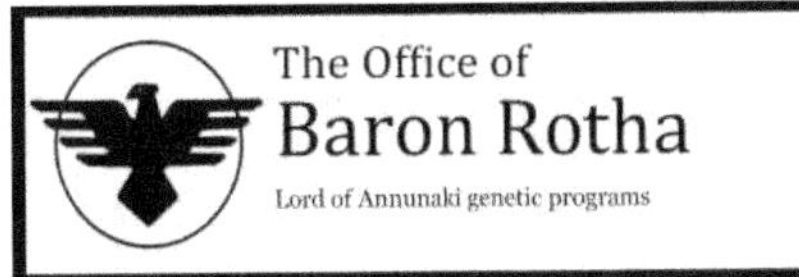

To Kin

(Reserved for your eyes only)

Your words now give me pause. My first will was to command every activity of the abomination. I see natural frequences as an impediment. The natural rhythms of life are more important than I first considered. I wonder to what extent my order is even possible.

I stand at a crossroads. The way has become less clear.

My eye is ever on the sun. The in-feeding current continues to increase in charge. The feeding current becomes more chaotic. The sun continues to increase in overall output. Mass ejections continue to increase in frequency. I fear the worst for our planet. I most dread the possibility of a full solar surface separation ejection. We can only imagine the decimation such a supernova would cause.

Therefore, speed this project. Therefore, increase the frequency of genius and epiphany in your work. Do whatever you can to find the answer. But make the abomination command-able.

To Baron Rotha

(Reserved for your eyes only)

I spoke to an Igigi pilot as it delivered supplies to my lab. It reported the C+ stripe of our Saturn has become more turbulent. It reported that it no longer makes deliveries to the gold atomization platform. Has the disperser platform been completed?

To Kin

(Reserved for your eyes only)

The disperser platform is near completion. Initial tests confirm its ability to atomize and disburse gold. Initial tests estimate monoatomic gold will stay suspended in the C+ band at 90% for 300+ years. The machinery is successful. There is some debate about monoatomic golds ability to form a hyper-toroidal current around the entire C+ band. There is no debate about its ability to catalyze and deflect solar radiation.

All eyes are on us to produce the gold.

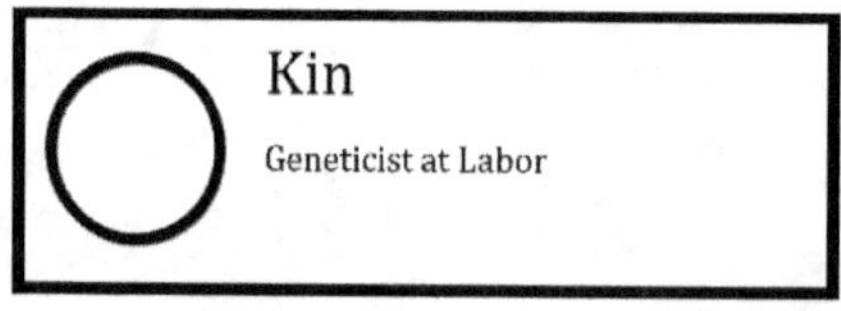

To Baron Rotha

(Reserved for your eyes only)

I had a dream. My thoughts turned to the gentle forests of our planet. I was standing on the edge of a cliff. Our purple sky glowed gently above. I felt a fearful emanation. The sky let out a groan. The opaque atmosphere of Saturn parted. Our hidden planet was revealed to space. The sun roared down. Then the forest burst aflame. The slime melted off the trees. The gel bushes turned into brown water. Everything burned.

I wish that the Igigi had completed their task. But I understand their refusal of such body-breaking work.

In the dream I saw the future of the abomination. Their skin sweats under the yellow sun. They sweat and toil. But they can endure it. They become angry. The back-breaking work only causes them to labor harder. Again and again they strike the earth with their tools.

A question seems to burn at the edge of my mind. It has not yet come into clear focus.

The abomination must feed, clothe and house itself. It must breed and raise the next generation of laborer. These activities will take the largest share of their time and attention. In hindsight, both you and Tar are more correct than I. The abomination must keep its love and social nature intact. I must have a very light touch when manipulating such motivations.

A dozen questions pursue me. What if groups of abomination escape? What if they flee the mine and move away? What if their numbers multiply exponentially?

What if new arriving species make alliance with them? What if the Saurians command them?

What of the native Terrans? I have heard no word about the Saurians. Certainly they are fully aware of our activities. Why do they not take an interest?

I must understand the life and society the abominations are to lead. Can you help bring focus to my anxieties?

To Kin

(Reserved for your eyes only)

They must not escape or command themselves. They must not be commanded by others. We do not spend such tremendous resources for the benefit of others. We do not spend the precious blood of so many priests for any cause except the Anunnaki.

I am convinced that they must retain the love and instinct of their group. You must not delay or confuse these instincts to any great extent.

Consider this saying of the kings of old, "no one can rule every man, but you can rule all men." If they are ruled as a group they will labor as a group. If they labor as a group we have succeeded. If they fear as a group we have succeeded. If they desire as a whole we have succeeded.

If the motivation of the group is our goal, what group motivations can we manipulate. List them.

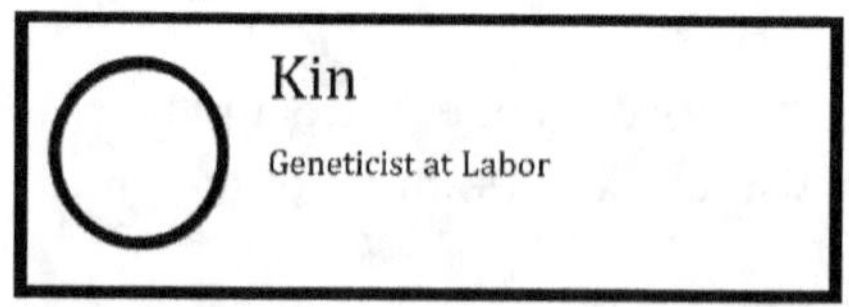

To Baron Rotha and Chief Priest Tar

Here I have compiled a list of possible social motivations.

1. ENCOURAGING: Love expressed as a reward, such as praising a toddler for walking.
2. FEARFUL REPRIMAND: Angry domination for failure or misdeed.
3. CAST AWAY: Shunned from the group, cut off from a relationship. Such as exile, divorce, fired from a job, demoted from status or rank.
4. HONORS PROMISED: Status expected if you join a group, such as a military or sporting team. Status promised if you accomplish.
5. HONORS SOUGHT: A dream of honors or rank attained by accomplishment.

I can intensify, minimize or confuse the above motivations. I further break social motivations down to personal elements.

1. SEEKING: This may be a vague emotion or a focused goal.
2. JEALOUSY: This emotion takes two forms.
   A. ENVY: The desire to destroy or stop what another possesses. Envy focuses on what is honored or possessed.
   B. DESIRE: To own, control or enjoy what others possess.
3. SOCIAL FEAR: Of being dishonored, rejected, criticized or exiled.
4. PRIMAL FEAR: Of violence, intimidation or an outpouring of rage.
5. COMFORTING: To aid self or another to return to comfort.
6. INSPIRING: To convince another, to create honors in the mind of another, to create desire in the heart of another.

All these motivations are social in nature and rooted in mammalian social patterns. I have attempted to experiment with these fundamental drives. I conclude that instinct resists manipulation. It seem to have a root deeper than genetics.

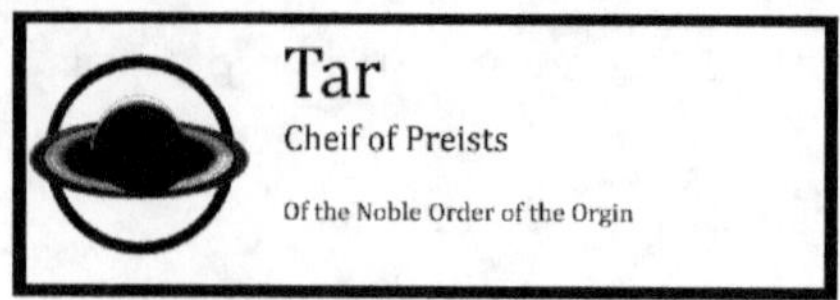

To Kin and Baron Rotha

I will elucidate and add to your list. There exists a prime motivation. It is the foundation of all motivations. The prime drive is *to experience.*

The Origin-mind projects into the material realm. It receives our new and unique experience. Our experience is food for the Origin-mind. No motivation is greater than the drive to experience. All life participates. All life is an emanation of the Origin-mind.

The actual matter of the physical domain has its own weak and primal consciousness. But this weak consciousness is undigestible to the Origin-mind.

The emanations of the Origin-mind probe the physical domain. A transformation occurs. Primitive physical consciousness fuses with ours. Because we are emanations of the Origin-mind a transformation occurs. The Origin-mind can then assimilate the transformed consciousness. The Origin-mind transforms and digests consciousness.

In our galaxy the Blue Avians traverse the stars in immense library ships. They seed proto-planets with the bacteria and fungi needed to create an atmosphere.

When the planet is ready, they return to seed it with every form of life which might survive. They depart. They let life 'fight it out.' The surviving creatures create the living biosphere. We ourselves are the progeny of the survivors of the fight.

As every planet is a forge of new species, they return periodically to gather new additions into their genetic library. They weed out harmful species.

They add and modify life forms. They, as it were, 'weed the garden and trim the tree.'

When a biosphere is ready, sentient beings are seeded. The hairy man of the forest was such a sentient seed. The hairy man of the forest was the second sentient type seeded on the Earth. The Blue Avians have given it a spark of proto-sentience. We assume they added a second sentient to the surface of the Earth because the Saurians have permanently withdrawn to their cities underground.

The All-man is the pattern for every bipedal intelligent species. The All-man contains all possibilities for every type of bipedal sentient. Animals also have an arch-pattern for their type. Every beetle, moth and grasshopper is an expression of the All-insect.

I have given you a very basic summary of the common scriptures for a reason. You seek to manipulate basic motivations. You must understand where these motivations fit in the overall scheme.

Most of the motivations you list are *of the animal*. They are the social instincts of animals. The All-man must contain the animal in order to survive. Animal instincts, such as child rearing and pack hierarchy are vital. They must not be impeded.

You must not meddle with survival instincts. The abomination must live, eat, reproduce and grow. You express a desire to manipulate these basic motivations. They are of the animal. Be very cautious to change them from their natural run.

Now do you understand the foundation of my argument?

See Attached Scriptures

Common scripture: The words of Samjapoo

Chapter 5, Paragraph 25

Upon the last twilight of redrim, I Samjapoo, bore the fever of a flu which near shook me from the mortal coil. I traveled, or perhaps was taken, by some kind of mysterious wind. There I met a being, tall and blue. His face resembled a bird, his skin a very fine feather, almost imperceptible feathers. His frame was similar to mine, except more ridged and slim. His eyes had the look of a predator. His entire physicality told of lethality. But his manner was warm. I saw a hint that love shone brightly behind his austerity. He spoke directly to the understanding of my mind.

He made a name that I can know him by. The understanding was, that I could not pronounce or even imagine his true name. His name was Zebrebeth. He communicated thus:

"Behold, I Zebrebeth find you. As you wander without map or aim, I find you. You a wanderer of the galactic roads, a mis-traveler of the tunnels of the either. Here inside the rainbow circle tunnel, I intercept you. And you are full of wonder and questions."

"I save you from disaster. I pull you from danger. Our city-ship approaches. You wander in the way, disaster pending. I pull you to safety. Such is my task and vigil. Not the first such soul to wander in the road."

"Here you are welcome. For a short while I will answer the wonder of your mind. We have no secrets here. But what is beyond your comprehension is rightly out of reach."

Here Zebrebeth began to show me, and what I saw was wonderous. If the scene before my eyes was a mystery he would explain.

First I saw the immensity of the ship. To say it is a city-ship is too modest. No city I know can approach its size. Beside a silvery band around the middle, and silvery caps on top and bottom, all exterior and interior walls were translucent. Every machine, implement and living being was visible.

Chapter 17, Paragraph 5

We left the library of genes and living flesh and living (morphogenetic) water. As we left, a question lighted on my mind. What is the number of creatures in your library? His answer, "That which is ever changing cannot be counted."

I wondered what destination the ship headed for. Instantly we appeared in the planning room. The next project was underway. Three of his peers hovered in the air, cross legged. They meditated, eyes open, fully aware and present. I was not given to fully understand their thoughts. Zebrebeth gave a summary. His communication, somehow, included parts of the thoughts of the three.

A rim of yellow flickered around a dull red-giant sun. It was understood that this sun would brighten and become yellow and smaller. This is backward to certain theories of solar evolution. An immense gas-giant planet orbited close to the sun. The sun poured out iron atoms in all directions. The gas-giant planet fed on them.

Something swirled just under the gas-giant's vaporous surface. Plasma currents snaked out from the core of the planet. The invisible currents took a form like a plasma globe. The currents slithered and jumped as they moved outward to the surface of the dusty atmosphere. Clumps of iron and nickel had coalesced under the atmospheric surface. If the clump moved at a certain speed it would continue to orbit just under the surface of the atmosphere. If the forming clump was too fast or too slow it would fall onto the core. If the clump grew large enough it would be ejected. Then it would be called a moon. From there it would draw mass to itself gravitationally. If it became large enough it might fly free of the super-Jupiter. It might become a rocky terrestrial planet.

One large clump held promise. It was larger than all the other clumps. It held a steady plasma current from the planet's core. Its magnetic field pulled in charged particles from every direction. Iron and other elements fed the growing clump.

The three Blue Avians held a giddy excitement. The excitement was mixed with love. They hoped for the future of this forming planetoid. But there was an argument between them. They all agreed that a certain iron eating bacteria needed to be seeded onto the planetoid. But they disagreed which strain was most optimal. The disagreement increased to the intensity of a war or a bar room brawl. But the love and harmony between the three was greater than the argument.

Chapter 325, Paragraph 76

Leaving the red-giant sun did not bring a feeling of accomplishment or rest. The opposite feeling shot throughout the ship. I understood that absolutely everyone was focused on the next stop. I also understood that the journey there would take many years.

The destination had been visited long ago. Not one of the avians was alive the last time the planet was visited. But the ship had been there. No time was wasted. They all took part in preparation.

They called it planet Zed-two. It was a rocky inner planet of a yellow sun. It was covered completely in water the last time it was visited. They expected it to have dried out by now. No one alive had seen it. No one had any direct information about it. All their current information was history, speculation and knowledge of the evolution of planets.

But they did have seers. Those with special sight had aggressively looked after this planet. Every vision and understanding of the seers became the talk of the ship. Everyone understood that seers are not perfect. Everyone understood that seers only interpret what is otherwise unknowable. It was even understood that when they arrive the planet might have been destroyed. Planet Zed-two might have fallen into the sun long ago. But they didn't believe it had. They assumed it was ready to seed.

Seeding is the most exciting event for the Avians. It brings more discussion and argument than any other task. Zed-two had, assumedly, developed a livable atmosphere and a rudimentary biosphere. Bacteria, fungi and phytoplankton were planted during the last visit. It was anticipated that over many thousands of years the microbes had terra-formed the planet. Now every phylum of organism could be seeded. The debate was over which organisms would be released.

The stop at Zed-two would last a very long time. Many older Avians expected they would spend the rest of their lives at Zed-two. To seed a planet with complex life forms involves many transitional phases. The life forms would be created on the ship as they approached. They would be released as the planet's environment evolved. The ship would only depart when life had stabilized and its success was assured.

I inquired about sentient life forms. The answer felt briskly dismissive. Zebrebeth was already engrossed in preparation for the seeding. He informed me sentient beings would be planted on another visit.

To Chief Priest Tar and Kin

I follow your most excellent summary.

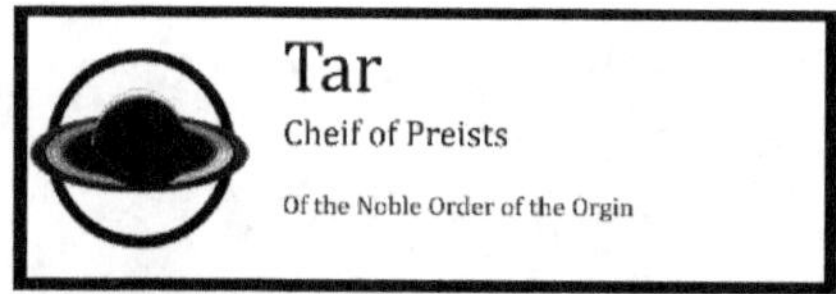

To Barron Rotha and Kin

Now, fully centered in the proper knowledge, I can give my perspective.

It is a saying among the priests, "Now you are lost in the academic." This means you are trying too hard to categorize and understand in terms of words.

Try another approach. The abomination is mostly the hairy man of the forest. The hairy man of the forest is mostly an animal. We assume the Blue Avians are preparing the hairy king of primates. They may one day fully infuse it with the All-man. We assume that a million years hence, if the hairy man of the forest is successful, the Blue Avians will give it full sentience. But you have done this very prematurely.

We are all aware that you could not succeed by splicing genes from your library. We know, that in desperation, you spliced your own genes with

the hairy man of the forest. This abomination of genetics is debated hotly
at every table. If our cause was not so urgent you would face punishment
for abomination. But your risk did succeed.

You have created a workable slave. You have created a viable servant being.
Do not suppose you can manipulate this happy accident without end. It
was fate that a slave laborer was even possible.

Look to the hairy beast of the forest. Look to yourself. These are the
motivations you have to work with. You will not manipulate their genetics
much further. The more you meddle, the more likely that you will only
make a mess.

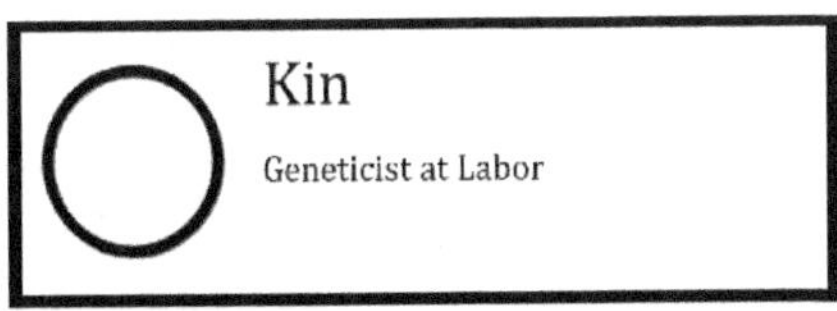

To Baron Rotha

(Reserved for your eyes only)

Tears escaped my eyes. At first Tar's words stung me. But I have recovered.
My resolve is renewed. I believe genetic manipulation is the ultimate way. I
believe the disorderly and lazy abomination can be genetically
manipulated. I can create a prototype to accomplish your command.

To Kin

(Reserved for your eyes only)

The Priests words have also stung my heart. I have not recovered.

Consider the ways in which we ourselves are motivated. Consider the ways in which the Earth mammals are motivated. I believe you can accomplish my command in another way. Let us explore social manipulations. Social manipulations will put less burden on genetics. Every change of biology brings a host of unintended consequences. Let us question now the motivation structure both we and the beasts share.

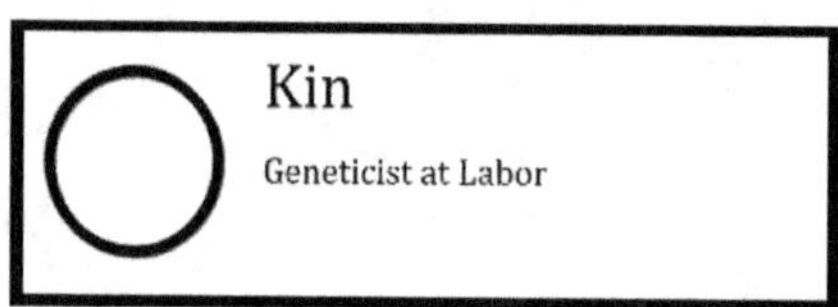

To Chief Priest Tar and Baron Rotha

I take your words to heart. I ponder the motivations of the beast.

 I am familiar with their ways of family and tribe. I have not pondered reproduction as a vector of control. I will consider it.

I have not yet seen a solution in any of their motivations. I have hope of finding a social motivation to accomplish the order. But I have not yet found a starting point.

To Kin and Chief Priest Tar

We have a direction. We will approach motivation as a social force. We are the same in our culture. We work for that which is social. The abomination will be likewise affected.

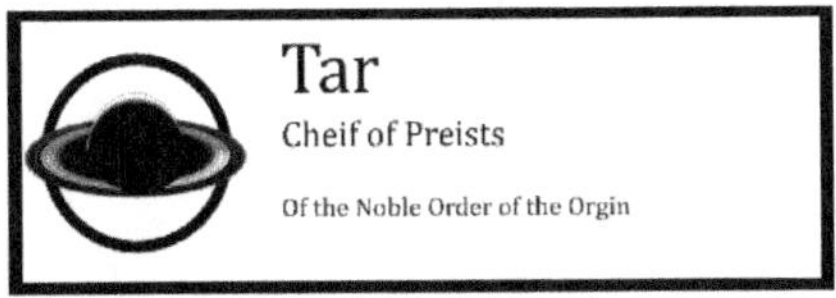

To Baron Rotha and Kin

Social motivations might fulfill your original command. Our people are lazy. Our people seek comfort first. Our people seek the easy thrills of cyber-sleep. They are unfocused in mind and action until socially motivated. Our productivity is only unlocked by social convention and institution.

Only those who seek union within the All-man can find any motivations which are not animal or social.

Let us continue to inquire of the social nature of motivation. Such inquiry is gainful to all.

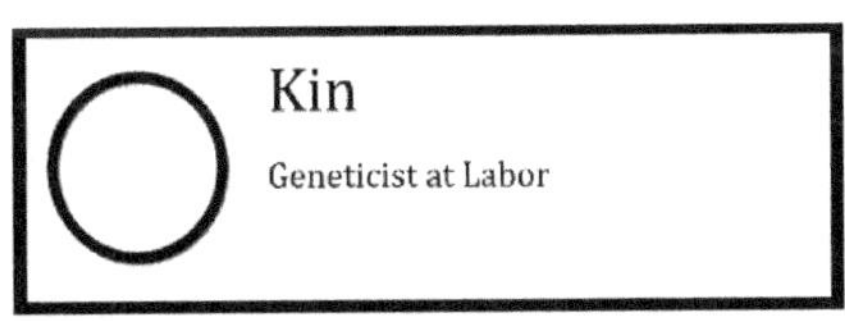

To Baron Rotha and Chief Priest Tar

I do what I do for unreasonable reasons. The success of this project will not elevate my status from Kin to Royal Family. I have no children to pass on an elevated name. I act by order, as I have been trained my entire life.

My personal will only comes alive when I am in my lab creating. There in my lab I am king, even god.

In the pantheon of the royal court I am no one. I am only called Kin as a formality. No actual blood relation binds me. I lack even the hope that my success will be rewarded with an office and a seal.

So I can't say much about my personal motivations.

To Kin and Chief Priest Tar

I write to advance our mission. But also as a personal purge and confession. I act as I was raised and trained. I serve the missions I am assigned. My personal will only comes alive when I am commanding. My personal will only comes alive when I am contending for a mission. But my will is confined within the limits of the assignment.

I fight to honor and maintain my seal. I strive to honor and maintain my family's position. Saying so, I see that most of my motivations are social. Like you Kin, my personal will comes alive when I am in my job.

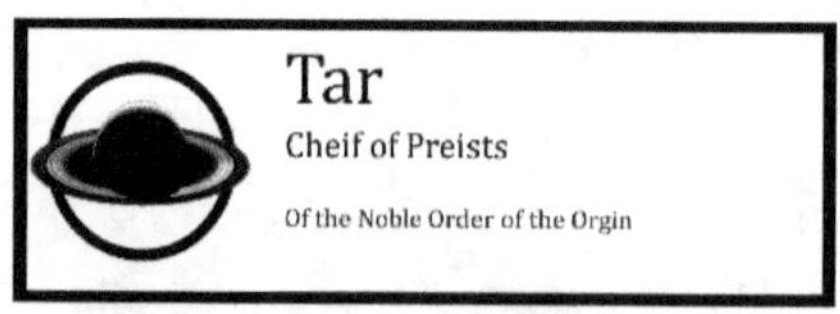

To Baron Rotha and Kin

I contribute as a matter of self-contemplation. When I study I become part
of the mind of the author. When I pray or when I actively inquire of the
universe, I become part of what is outside of myself. My center disappears.

Strangely, when I attempt to contact the All-man I feel only myself. When
I attempt to merge with the All-man I often feel a subtle frustration. I feel
a failure and incompleteness. I have pondered on this. Is this the nature of
the All-man or only a reflection of myself?

I have a seal and an office. I spend much of my time directing others.
Much of my time I spend overseeing the operation of the institute.

I feel alive at the times my attention is quiet. At all other times, what I feel
is a variety of irritations.

Now I feel compelled to ask, if your current abomination can use our tools
and understand our commands, then what more is lacking? Why is it not
enough?

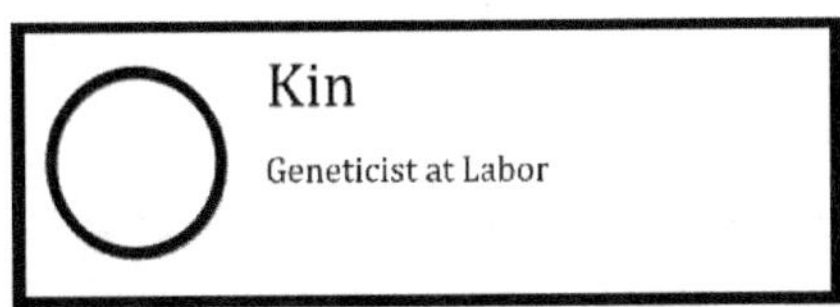

To Baron Rotha and Chief Priest Tar

As we correspond it occurs to me, the foundation of motivation is to gain
something which one does not have. Even prayer and study seek that
which we do not possess. Every project seeks a result not presently
enjoyed. Therefore, all motivation is simply hunger for what one does not
have.

I need to discover what the abomination does not have. As they live in the
facility, all their needs are provided for.

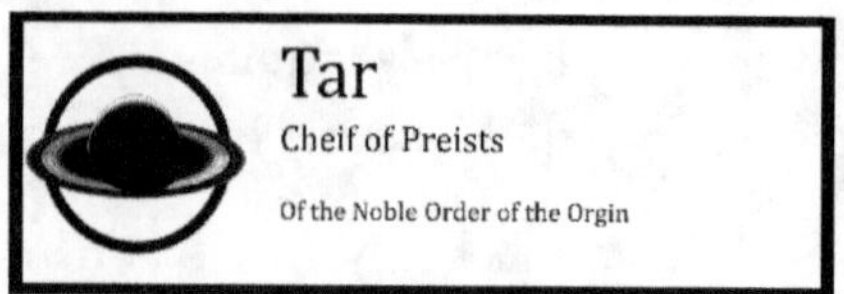

To Kin and Baron Rotha

As each sentient species is only an incomplete fragment of the All-man, we hunger for its wholeness. We wish to express those parts not included in our species. The All-man is an extension of the Origin-mind. Some pause here to argue that the All-man is itself incomplete. This debate is far from settled. What is clear is that the Origin-mind entered this domain to feed. Therefore, nothing is more fundamental than hunger.

To Kin and Chief Priest Tar

Now we have a clear view of the background and nature of our task. Our primary motivations are social. Our prototype is closer to ready than we assumed. We are capable of genetically modifying the hungers and needs of the abomination. But it is best to do so as little as possible. Now provide a list of social aspects which might be used.

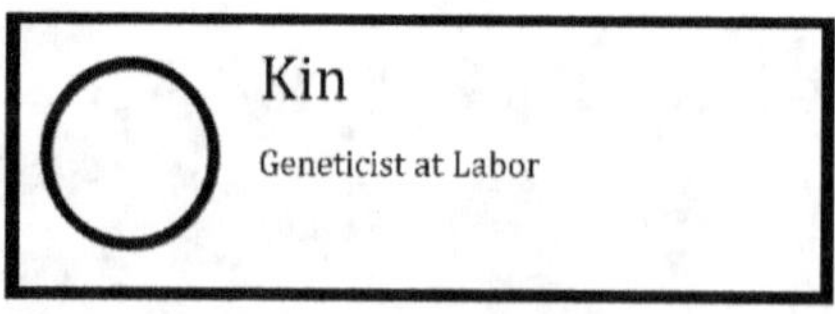

To Baron Rotha and Chief Priest Tar

I note that the abomination divides its time in much the same way as its mammal cousins. Its priorities are: first play and comfort, second food, third hierarchy and last breeding.

They put fierce energy into play. Even more aggregate energy than hierarchy or seeking a mate. If we could harness their energy of play we would command the most powerful slave force in the galaxy. If we could command this energy they would outperform the Igigi by a factor of sixteen.

But I must quench these ambitions. My latest prototype has not been greatly successful. I did correct problems of excessive physical strength and aggression in the males. In earlier prototypes I concluded that male aggression caused excessive damage to each other. This was solved simply by optimizing the timed release of testosterone. I also solved a problem with excessive sexual receptivity in females. Their receptivity was causing excessive competition in the males. It was also causing an excessive reproduction rate.

Despite these small successes, they have not been productive workers. They do understand our command. They can use our tools. Some of them understand the overall aim of mining. But as soon as the Igigi leave they become unproductive.

Only one-hundred Igigi remain loyal to me. Only ten are on duty at any time. This is far below the number needed to lead a sufficient workforce. Therefore, this prototype is a failure.

To Kin and Chief Priest Tar

Royal leadership meetings focus on the Igigi strike and little else. Our relationship with our esteemed work partners has lasted over six-hundred thousand years without major interruption.

It would be an extraordinary benefit to all Anunnaki if the abomination could do the difficult labor. The Igigi would then do the more technical work. If you can give me demonstrated hope of abomination super-productivity I will call out to all royals. They will provide every resource. They will hold nothing back.

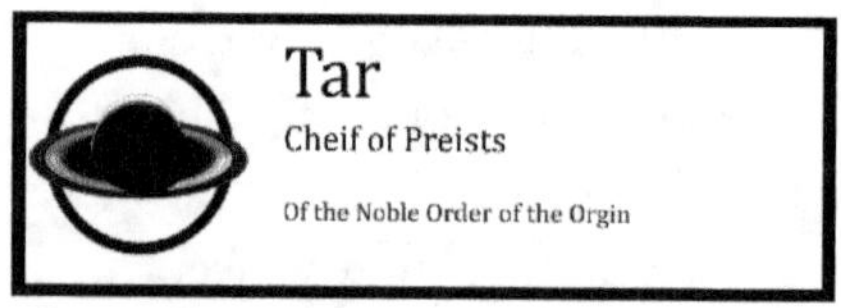

To Kin and Baron Rotha

Let me again insert the perspective of the All-man. The abomination requires the soul of a priest to enlighten it. Thereby it is proven that the abomination shares the All-man. If the abomination is an emanation of the All-man, even a greatly limited emanation, then ask, what would be fitting of our people and our very selves? Do not be arrogant because the abomination has a confused brain. Do not be arrogant because the abomination was given a symbolic and arbitrary language. What you demand of the abomination; ask, is it fitting of any emanation of the All-man?

To Kin and Chief Priest Tar

If we assume them somewhat similar to ourselves, can we establish a system of royal hierarchy and family position? Can we grade them based on family accomplishment?

To Baron Rotha and Chief Priest Tar

They are too chaotic for our social system. They reproduce chaotically so family lines become mixed. Their genes continually mix and adapt. I modify their genes frequently.

They fight and kill each other frequently. Royal family members would be a target for usurpers. They share resources arbitrarily. They withhold or steal resources arbitrarily. When my Igigi teach them a social practice they soon break or change that practice.

For these reasons I have sought a genetic based motivation and command.

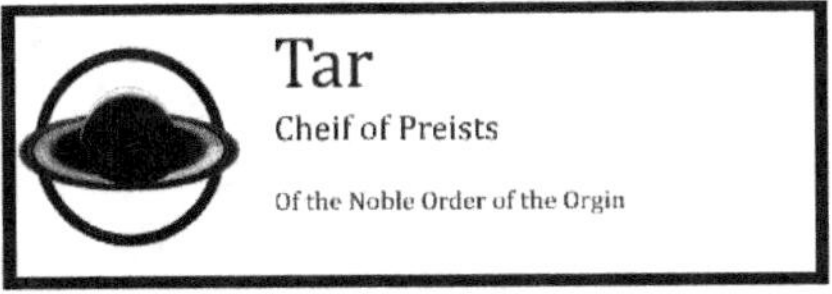

To Kin and Baron Rotha

A cursory knowledge of history reveals primitive cultures have often used a prize system. A medallion or other rare object is traded. The prize object may be exchanged for goods or favors.

Some primitive cultures have used items of utility for trade. Storable food or building materials have acted as items of exchange.

Consider such a prize system for the abomination.

To Chief Priest Tar and Kin

As our sole purpose is to mine gold, if it proves effective, let gold be the prize. Let the abomination hold a small portion of refined gold as the prize.

Further, if it is possible, modify the abomination genetically to value gold. Such will serve a dual purpose. They will mine for the love of gold. They will also trade gold for goods and favors.

We will distribute gold to them as a prize for mining. We will reward them for obeying our command with gold. Can such a fascination with gold be written into their genes?

To Baron Rotha and Chief Priest Tar

I do not know of any natural gene which loves gold. Certain birds have an affinity for shiny objects.

Maybe a love of gold can become an instinct. I only have a cursory knowledge of instinct. The mental domain is not my field of expertise. If instinct is the crossroads of genetics, environment and experience then we need an expert in the experiential sciences.

Now that we touch on the subject, I wonder, does architecture create instinct in a people over time? Does art influence instinct over time? Does education and vocation build an instinct over time? I have not pondered the development of instinct over many generations.

Priests and the ruling class may have a better understanding of the manipulation and maintenance of instinct. Because the priest and royals maintain the common mind of our people, they would be the ones to ask.

To Dutchess Shera, Chief Priest Tar and Kin

I have called Dutchess Shera of the Royal Family to our dialogue. As an esteemed inner member of the Royal Family, in perfect standing, she reports directly to the Royal Council. I welcome her to our group dialogue.

Our task is to answer the following question: can we program the abomination with the instinct to value, desire and peruse gold? Can such an instinct be impressed and maintained. We solicit your royal comment.

To Chief Priest Tar and Baron Rotha

CC: Associates

The Royal Family hears your call. We are aware of your project. We have given permission for the Duke of Projects to support your efforts. I have come to oversee your progress. I have reviewed your correspondence.

As our people have evolved away from primitive systems of motivation, as our people live only to serve the Royal Monarch and the Royal Monarch lives only to serve the greatness of our people, therefore this question is fit for an anthropologist of primitive cultures.

Tar, Chief of Priests, what say the uncommon scriptures of base and primitive motivations? Search diligently for an insightful answer.

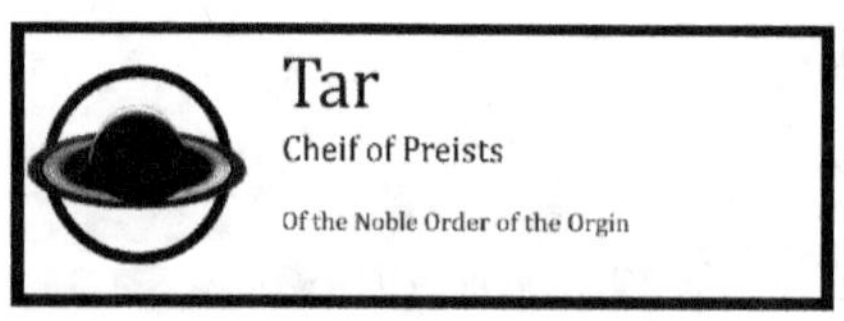

To all

From a lifelong search of all available scripture, it is the shared opinion of most priests, that *all people* fall to the base and primitive motivations. We therein ignore the manifold possibilities of the All-man. We all fall to the base side of our animal nature.

Our people have fallen. Most of the Anunnaki spend most of their lives in cyber-sleep. And in cyber-sleep commit every sin; lewd and bizarre sex, violence of all imaginable kinds, drunkenness in every way the mind can be twisted. Every sin, in its essence, has been made a building block. From blocks of sin our people create worlds, then delight to invite each other to visit.

So little is accomplished in cyber-sleep. Even the forums of science fall to fruitless argument. Even the forums of science fall to gangs of squabbling banter. The typical arguments are those which cannot be settled by experiment or reason, therefore they are fruitless.

It is the opinion of most priests that our people are motivated, almost entirely, by the primitive and base. With all due respect.

To Baron Rotha

(Reserved for your eyes only)

Delete Chief Priest Tar from our dialogue. Tar is irrelevant.

To Dutchess Shera

(Reserved for your eyes only)

It will be done as you command.

To Kin

(Reserved for your eyes only)

By order of Dutchess Shera, Chief Priest Tar is to be deleted from future correspondence in this conversation.

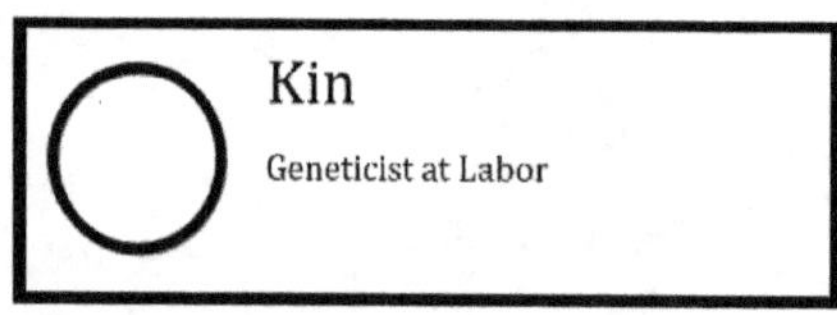

To Baron Rotha

(Reserved for your eyes only)

Understood. In this conversation with you and Shera I shall delete Chief Priest Tar from future correspondence.

To Kin

(Reserved for your eyes only)

Address Dutchess Sherra with great respect and the upmost discretion.

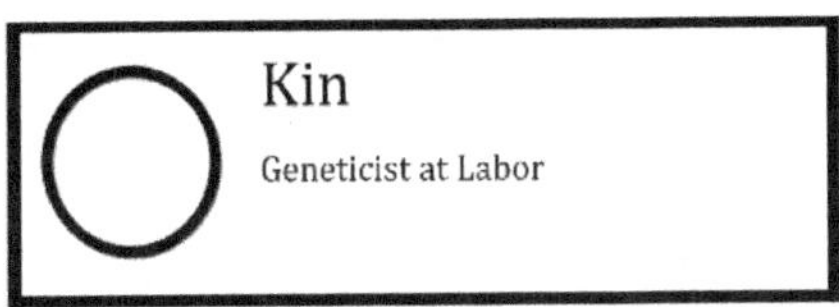

To Baron Rotha and Dutchess Shera

Inspired by previous communications, I have instructed my Igigi to appear in the form most impressive to the abomination. Disguised as glorious winged beings of light they gave out small discs of gold. The aim was to impress upon them the importance of gold.

I must report this as a failure. I disbursed the gold discs. Soon afterward they were forgotten, lost or even thrown like rocks.

The abomination needs an inborn instinct to revere gold. Otherwise I fear it will be no motivation to them.

To Baron Rotha

CC: Associates

Lord Rotha, I will receive communications from you directly and only from you, as you have rank and position in the extended Royal Family.

To Dutchess Shera and Kin

I have received a request for information from my subordinate. The question is: if gold fails as a motivation, what motivation shall be eminent?

To Baron Rotha

CC: Associates

The only motivation of value is to serve the King and the greatness of the Anunnaki people. Therefore the abomination are beasts. As unworthy beasts they have no motivation, but only hungers. Let them dance for their dinner. Let them produce an allotment of gold ore or they will not be fed.

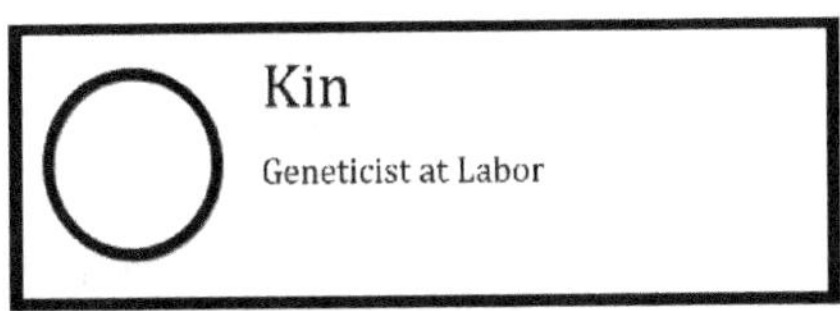

To Baron Rotha

CC: Royal Associates

My calculations are sure. We lack sufficient number of Igigi. The abomination must manage the mine. They must also manage agriculture and child rearing. Gold production can only be sufficient if the abomination primarily lead themselves. We created them because machines operated by our few Igigi are insufficient. We must motivate them. They must understand their tasks and perform continuously. We do not have the resources to supervise them closely. If our project fails then the solar nova will ravage our planet.

To Dutchess Shera and Kin

Is the failure complete? Are there no abomination which crave gold to the smallest degree? Are there not even a few who could become the stock of a new prototype?

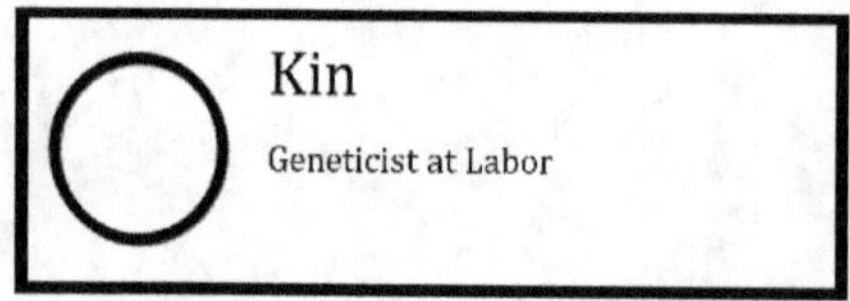

To Baron Rotha

CC: Royal Associates

The abomination are driven by a chaotic heart and mind. They have a great variety of drives and motivations. They go to great lengths to distinguish themselves among their group. The abomination crave individuality. They go to great lengths to distinguish their uniqueness.

There are a few which somewhat crave gold. But they are hoarders. They hoard everything. They are not good at laboring or at leading labor.

To Kin and Dutchess Shera

Then you have answered the question yourself. The abomination respond to a multitude of motivations. Therefore create a system of multiple overlapping motivations. List the possibilities you have observed in this latest prototype.

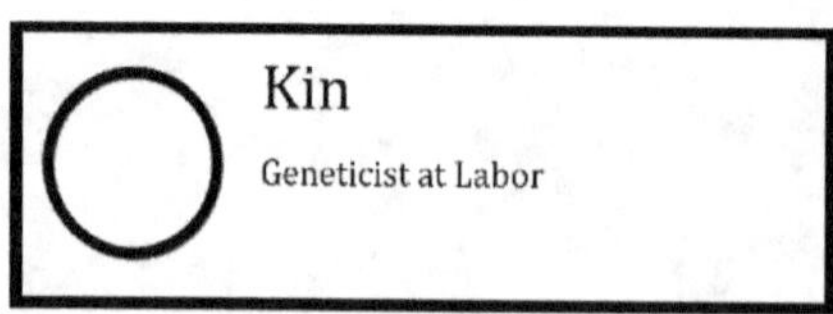

To Baron Rotha

CC: Royal Associates

My first thought is always genetics. I cannot escape the belief that genes are the path to produce a consistent and steady product. I still hope for a genetic solution because of the ever changing focus of abomination society.

But as you command, I often secretly observe the abomination. Lately I have watched with an eye to social motivations.

Most abomination strut like birds. The men strut their strength. The women strut their beauty and sexiness. The youth strut their energy. Even the stupid strut their stupidity. They respond to each other's display with either adoration or enmity. Whatever they strut others will love or hate. Whatever they strut others will seek to possess and control or even jealously tear down.

When I gave out gold discs, the ones which gained them were the focus of jealous attention. Others gathered around and desired to hold what they themselves did not possess.

But they are a chaotic species. They soon lose interest. Most of the gold discs were soon abandoned. A few hoarders gathered them up and hid them.

I do not see a way to use this social characteristic as motivation.

To Baron Rotha

CC: Associates

Your only option is to develop a money economy. A primitive and chaotic species cannot operate by any other principle.

To Dutchess Shera and Kin

How shall money become motivation? Does it relate to the abomination strutting around?

To Baron Rotha

CC: Associates

Money is limited in supply and therefore exclusive. What one attains others shall desire. They must be made to work in order to attain what others possess.

The abomination is not capable of working for the King and the glory of the people. They cannot be satisfied with an allotment of food, shelter and what is necessary to continue work.

They are a chaotic species, a hungry species. They are a species driven by pride and selfish honors. Most of all, they are a simple minded species.

Therefore they must hold in their hand a symbol of greatness and good.
They must hold a golden symbol in their hand because they cannot hold
the good in their understanding.

To Kin and Dutchess Shera

Devise a money system to motivate the abomination. Advise me of your
progress.

To Baron Rotha

CC: Royal Associates

The abomination do not have the mental capacity to enact a system of
money. I limited their intelligence. Only a few of them can do more than
understand our commands and use our tools. They have been given a
confused and flighty brain. They have been given a symbolic language
without any natural foundation. If we give them greater intelligence they
will rebel like the Igigi.

I beg you to rescind the order. We will do well to find another solution.

To Kin and Dutchess Shera

Over five-hundred Earth years have passed since we began this project. The sun rebels against its boundaries. The sun shows a new and aggressive habit. Even now, the sun shows an intense increase in the frequency and intensity of coronal mass ejections. Even now average solar output soars. The sun has changed from gentle yellow to yellow-white. Even at this early junction our home and all other planets show a rise in surface temperature. Time is short. Our situation demands a new approach. Proceed.

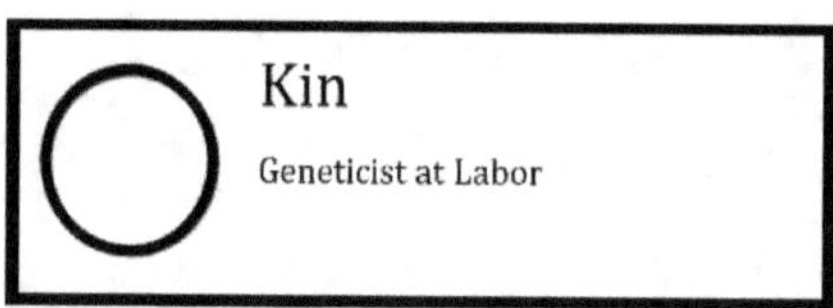

To Baron Rotha

CC: Royal Associates

I passed out golden discs. Only the hoarders kept them. My drones retrieved all the discs. As an escalation, my Igigi, costumed as a being of light, declared the glory of the golden discs. The result was the same. There was interest at the initial disbursement. Afterward the discs were ignored. Only the hoarders kept them. This program proves to be hopeless.

To Baron Rotha

CC: Associates

Inform your subordinate of the nature of want. Desire is that which one lacks. What is already possessed cannot be desired. The only hurdle yet to be achieved is to make the money rare and difficult to achieve. The only hurdle not yet traversed is to associate money with desires.

The money must be regarded as indistinguishable from virtue. The money must become equal to things the abomination strut. If beauty is strutted then beauty must be rewarded with money. In order to make money rare only the greatest beauty is to be rewarded.

Continue to develop the money system.

To Kin and Dutchess Shera

The task is to associate money with that which they strut. Generate a list of attributes the abomination strut. Create a list of ways each attribute may be rewarded with money.

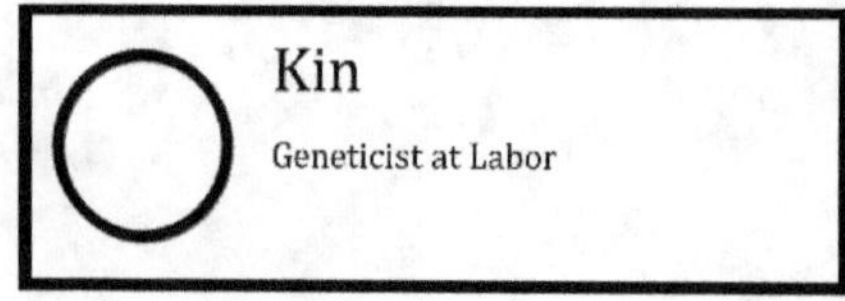

To Baron Rotha

CC: Royal Associates

I find myself lacking in this task. I begin with the attribute of beauty. How can it be rewarded? I follow with the attribute of strength. How can it be rewarded? Last, I consider the primary objective of work. How can it be rewarded with money?

To Kin and Dutchess Shera

Have the Igigi appear as beings of light. Let them judge the attributes of the abomination. Let it be rewarded with discs of gold.

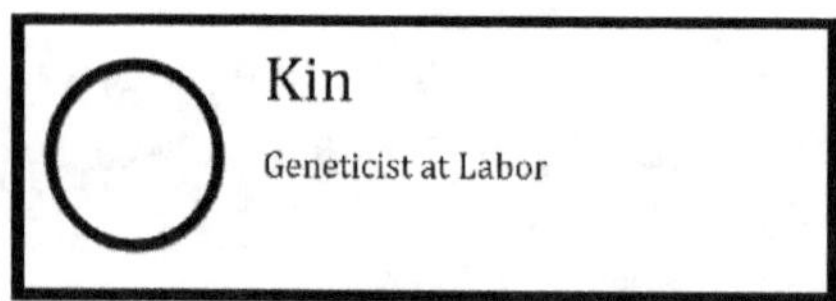

To Baron Rotha

CC: Royal Associates

I have done as commanded. The Igigi appeared. The judgements were made. The golden discs were bestowed as reward. The recipients were honored by all. The golden discs were held tightly for a day or two. Then they were abandoned and forgotten. The value of the reward is short lived. It also appears to me that there is no reason for the abomination to keep the reward after the shine of the honors have passed.

Additionally, if only the best workers are rewarded, I believe the rest of the abomination will refuse to work.

Dutchess Shera

Royal Dutchess of Karn

Superior of the
Royal Order of Saturn

To Baron Rotha

CC: Associates

Instruct your charge to withhold food from the abomination. After each abomination works all day give them a gold disc. For the best worker give two discs. Give food only in exchange for a gold disc. The best worker may keep the extra disc.

Kin

Geneticist at Labor

To Baron Rotha

CC: Royal Associates

After some trial and error the project has proven somewhat successful. Labor tasks were devised. The abomination were trained at task. They learned to expect a gold disc in exchange for a day's labor. They quickly learned a gold disc was necessary to be fed.

The problem is that the best workers are always the same few. They ignore the extra gold disc because their needs are met with one disk. The overall productivity of the abomination is low. They produced only a little above what a machine could produce. I believe this project has proven a failure.

To Baron Rotha

CC: Associates

I am delighted with the success of your money project. Additional productivity may be achieved by more clever incentive. Instruct your staff to provide three levels of food, clothing and housing. Let the higher producers use the money to attain a higher quality of each necessity.

To Kin and Dutchess Shera

Command your Igigi to construct and fabricate three graduations of food, clothing and housing. Reward labor by three gradations. The top third of producers receive triple the disc of the lower third of producers.

To Baron Rotha

CC: Associates

I began planning a similar scheme before your command arrived. I devised a plan of ten gradations. On further thought, I find your scheme is superior. The abomination are simple minded. It is most important that they understand the relation between labor and reward. Your triple gradation system is in progress.

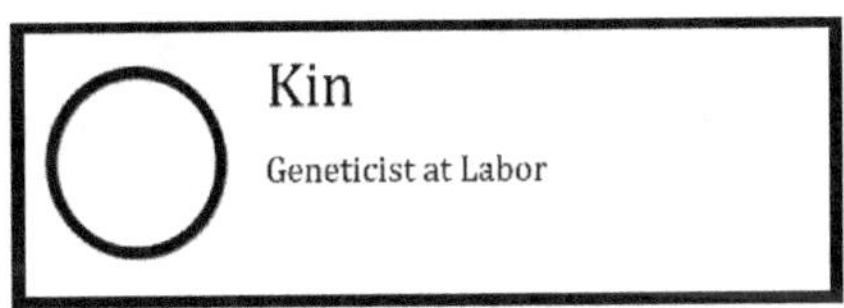

To Baron Rotha

CC: Royal Associates

I am pleased with the progress of this scheme. The abomination prove sufficiently productive. I have moved operations out of the lab. The abomination are now living on the surface. I am evaluating the possibility of beginning mining operations in the Absutu.

However I have a few recurrent difficulties. The lower third typically work very little. They are not motivated by the system. They know they can attain one disc with little work. They understand one disc is enough to satisfy their needs. They either do not wish to, or are incapable of, working hard enough to raise their position.

To Baron Rotha

CC: Associates

Instruct your charge to punish the lowest producers. Make a fourth category for a small fraction of the lowest producers. Deny them benefit. Give them shame and additional burdens. I defer to you to devise the punishment.

To Kin and Dutchess Shera

Let the lowest ten percent of workers suffer want and burden. Exclude those abomination too young to be competitive. Also exclude those with child or caring for children. Let those too old to work or too malformed be destroyed – discretely.

Produce a list of additional ways we may build upon the success of the system of gold disc reward.

To Baron Rotha

CC: Royal Associates

I have completed your gradation scheme. The lowest ten percent have been denied a meal. To maintain their calorie needs they are given additional calories in the other meals. Additionally, they have been given clothing which is irritating to their skin. The inferior clothing denotes their lowest social status.

I created a plan to discreetly destroy the old and malformed. I instructed the Igigi to appear as an angel of light. They were instructed to say, "I take this good person to a place of forever comfort and joyful amazement. You will see them no more until you are also old and taken to the place of joy."

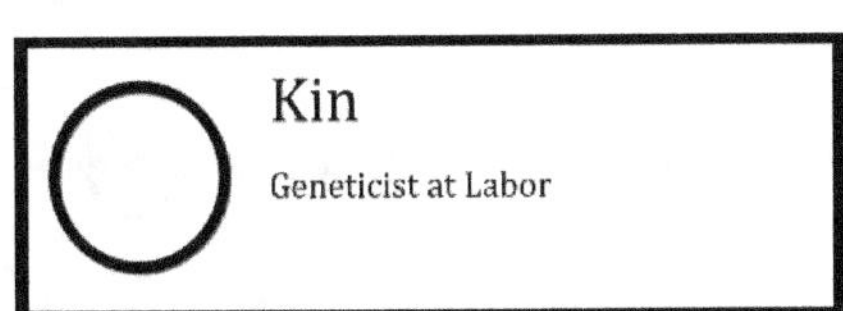

To Baron Rotha

CC: Royal Associates

I must report the fourth gradation has backfired. The lowest lose all hope. They produce even less. The punishment of the ten percent is a failure.

To Baron Rotha

CC: Associates

I commend the Igigi for their clever design against the old. But your subordinate lacks wisdom. The extra gradation is not a failure. There is only one failure here. Your subordinate fails to understand. The punishment is not for the motivation of the lowest ten percent. They are unimportant. It is the ninety percent of workers who will be motivated. They will work to avoid such a punishment. Additionally, the punishment of the lowest will add contrast which will elevate all the other grades.

To Kin and Dutchess Shera

Continue the course. I await your list of additional ways the disc system may be employed.

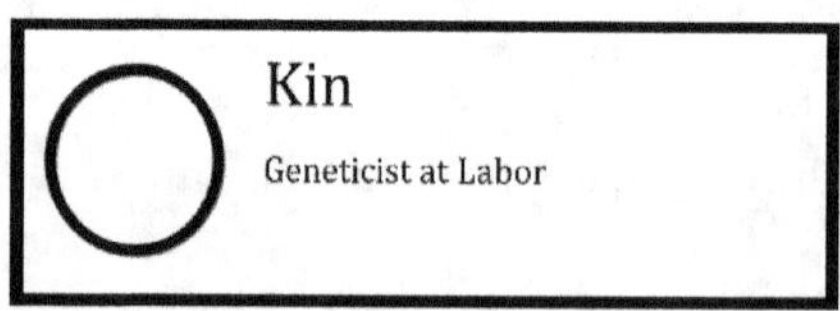

To Baron Rotha

CC: Royal Associates

I have a close view of the lowest ten percent. They stay in a wretched and shameful state. They did not occupy this awful state before the addition of the fourth gradation. It pains me to see them in perpetual shame.

To Baron Rotha

CC: Associates

Outrageous weakness has reached my attention. Each and every Anunnaki is bound by law and honor to give all to the King and the greatness of the Anunnaki people. The lack of honor of a lowly creature, such as the abomination, is of no concern to the Royal Family. The social esteem of the abomination is irrelevant to the greatness of the Anunnaki. I am outraged that such a trivial matter would even be expressed. Tighten your command. Make our priorities clear.

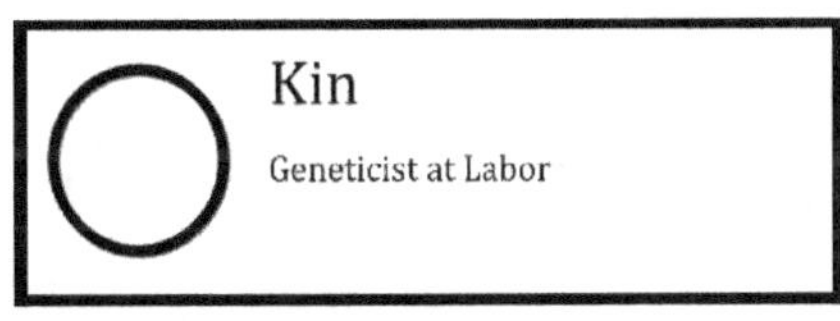

To Baron Rotha

CC: Royal Associates

By your command I pursue an understanding of further motivations as they relate to the system of gold discs. Hierarchy is a primary mammalian social motivation. I have expanded the existing reward system.

I have used housing as a social status. I instructed my Igigi to construct a grand and ornate house. The grand house is triple the size of the top gradation housing. Beside the grand house I constructed three other houses twice the size of the top gradation dwellings, but not as ornate as the grand house.

My goal was to establish an alpha house, after the alpha wolf or lion. The three nearby houses represent the challengers. Social mammals have an alpha and a few who threaten to take the alpha position. The alpha is forever pursued by a small group of challengers. Eventually the alpha will grow old or suffer injury. Then one of the challengers will take the role.

My cunning was to use alpha honors, naturally reserved for the strongest bruit, and give it to the most productive worker. I put the most productive worker and his family in the grand house. Brute mammal strength was replaced with productivity at labor.

As I conceived of this plan I regarded myself as greatly cunning and devious. In hindsight the plan is only common sense. The plan was presented by fate. It merely follows practical and natural principles.

This change is successful. Abomination from all gradations give the grand houses much attention. I have noted a general increase in productivity from all three main gradations.

However, abomination society has become more complex. It is impossible to tell if this new plan is the primary cause of the increase in productivity. I am now convinced this prototype is capable of performing in the Absutu. I am making preparations to greatly increase the population of abomination.

To Kin and Dutchess Shera

I am delighted to hear of your success. Mining the rich gold deposits in the south-most lands is ever on my mind. Let us not be hasty. Is this prototype capable of all functions of mining as well as surviving in the Absutu? What tests are needed to prove readiness?

To Baron Rotha

CC: Royal Associates

Our correspondence has mostly focused on motivation. But my constant focus, over the last six-hundred years, has been to build a strong and robust slave being. My criteria has always been that they should thrive under harsh natural environments. In this I have succeeded.

I request to move my operations from the middle lands of Earth to the gold rich Absutu of South Africa.

To Kin and Dutchess Shera

I am filled with delight by your request. You have been granted approval
to move operations to the Absutu. You have approval to set up mining
operations in the Absutu. All necessary resources are approved for your
needs. I salute your success. Keep me informed of your progress.

To Baron Rotha

(Reserved for your eyes only)

Great power is given to one without title. Is this Kin the best candidate to
lead this part of the project?

To Dutchess Shera

(Reserved for your eyes only)

I have worked closely with this Kin for over six-hundred years. His family
has no seal. His blood lines are from the middle lines of the riffraff. Yet he
is the best geneticist of all the Anunnaki. His genius is fate. He has no
rival. The project cannot succeed without him.

He unerringly obeys all my commands. He has managed the Igigi workers without flaw. He has managed both the facilities and the living stock. I trust him completely to continue this project.

To Baron Rotha

(Reserved for your eyes only)

As we move operations to the Absutu a new problem arises. I have not noticed it before because the abomination have been less than one hundred in number. They have always been constrained to a small area. Their activities have been closely directed.

Now they work in a larger area with less supervision. Now a type of troublemaker has arisen. Some of the abomination are sensitive to the All-man. A few of each generation are aware that they are an emanation of something spiritual. They disrupt the others with stories and realizations.

To Chief Priest Tar and Kin

We call you again for assistance. The abomination present a new trouble. We question how to deal with a divergent type. Some of the abomination show qualities somewhat reminiscent of the priestly class. They seem to have a knowing connection to the All-man. We question how to proceed.

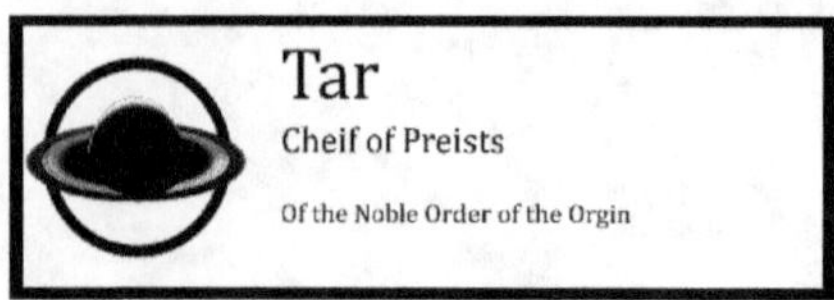

To Baron Rotha and Kin

All sentient beings have a knowing relation to the All-man. Most are too preoccupied to meditate on it. My priests are chosen because they show a natural affinity to understand the All-man. A few choose themselves because they desire to know the All-man. What you speak of is not a problem but rather a virtue.

To Chief Priest Tar and Baron Rotha

My concern grows. The abomination have more freedom in the Absutu. My Igigi are employed in technological projects. They have very little time to direct the abomination.

The abomination are capable of completing the assigned tasks. They are especially motivated to build new habitations and set up agriculture. They see the necessity of such projects. Leaders from among their ranks understand the tasks in detail. Leaders from their own ranks give orders and track progress. The work proceeds adequately.

A new social movement grows like a cancer. A new dialogue arises among the workers. A new idea takes many shapes. They do not know it as the All-man. They do not have a coherent philosophy to describe it. They do not have an institution to study and promote it. Instead they have a chaotic outpouring to express what they are blind to.

This social trend is growing. It robs focus from the work.

To Chief Priest Tar and Kin

We are on the edge of success. We cannot let anything stand in our way. We must find a way to refocus the abomination. Any perspective will be greatly appreciated.

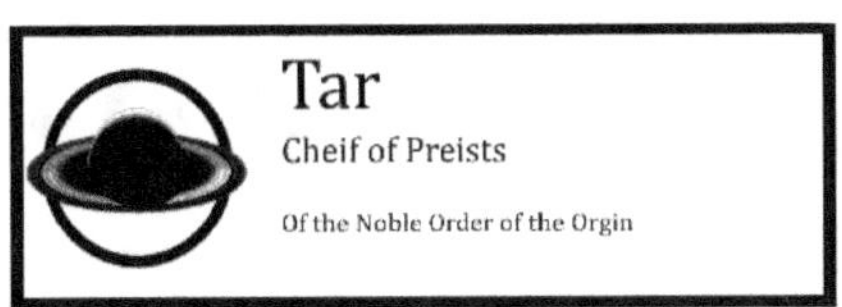

To Baron Rotha and Kin

The All-man is all. If you know the common scriptures you know this. You may know it in your intellect and ignore it in your whole being. The All-man is all. This is the heart of a priest.

You cannot shield a sentient being from their own self. The All-man is the self. The All-man is all. You cannot stop what is.

Awareness of the All-man is part of every society. This applies to the abomination.

To Kin

(Reserved for your eyes only)

This juncture is critical. The focus must remain on work. Tar has not given an answer. We must involve the Royal Family. Do not include Chief Priest Tar in the following correspondence.

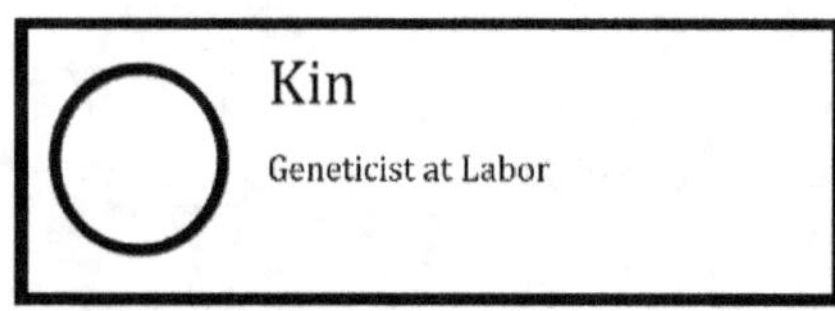

To Baron Rotha

(Reserved for your eyes only)

I hope this message reaches you in time. Please delay contacting Dutchess Shera. I need more time to find a solution.

To Kin

(Reserved for your eyes only)

What solution do you propose?

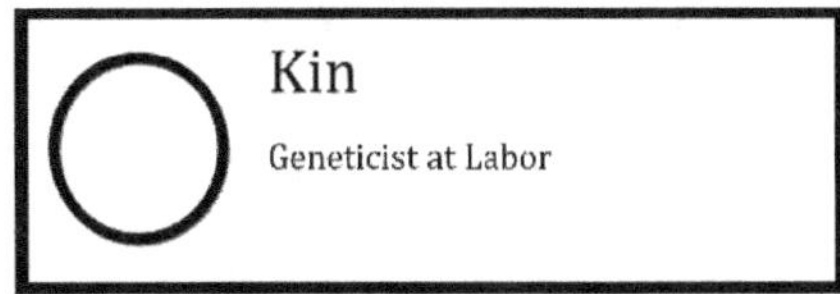

To Baron Rotha

(Reserved for your eyes only)

I am in the observation phase of research. I expect an epiphany soon.

To Kin

(Reserved for your eyes only)

The project cannot be endangered. We must enlist all available aid. I understand you have a close working relationship with those which you created. A more emotionally detached perspective may be a necessary. Standby for a dialogue with the Royal Family.

To Dutchess Shera and Kin

I request assistance with an abomination social problem. Certain of the abomination have developed spiritual sensitivity. Apparently their sensitivity is contagious. It is causing a disruption of focus. We are beginning production at the mine. At this critical juncture any disruption of focus could be injurious to our program.

To Baron Rotha

CC: Associates

Kill the sensitive individuals immediately. Remove them from the working gene reservoir.

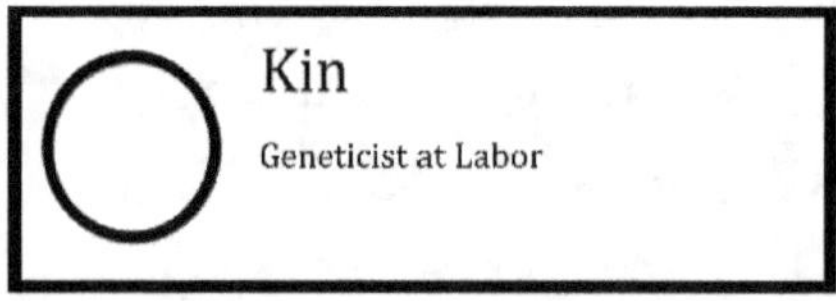

To Baron Rotha

CC: Royal Associates

To kill the sensitive was my first plan. But Tar explains it wisely, "You cannot shield a sentient being from their own self. The All-man is the self." I seek a social solution. I believe the ability is too widespread to kill every abomination with this sensitivity.

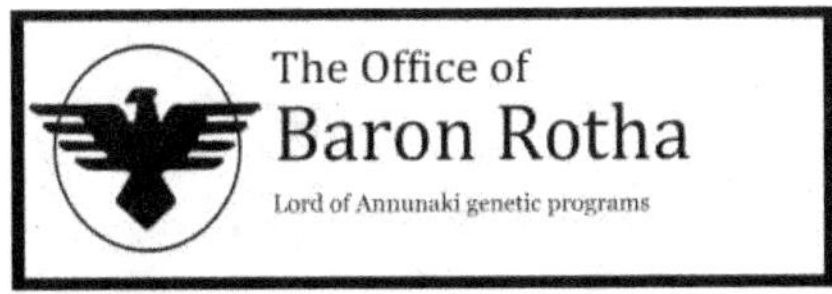

To Kin

(Reserved for your eyes only)

You did not inform me that you had attempted to weed out the sensitivity from the gene reservoir.

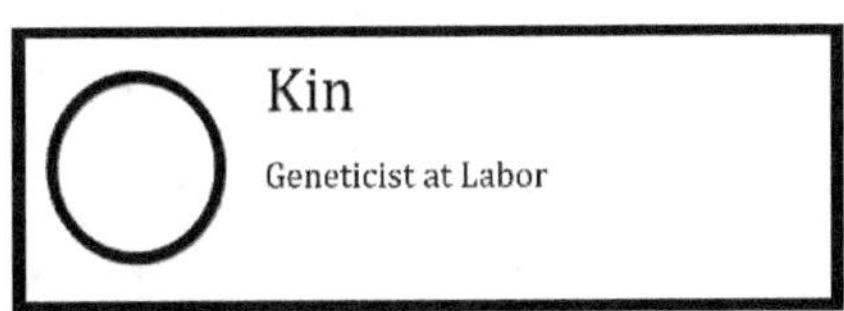

To Baron Rotha

(Reserved for your eyes only)

I stated precisely that it was my first <u>plan</u>. I made no statement of fact. I do believe that "killing the prophets" is not a long-term solution.

To Baron Rotha

CC: Associates

If you are unable or unwilling to root out the problem genetically, the only solution is to create a religion. I shall resolve your first possible inquiry. No, I do not mean to begin a holy institute such as our priests.

The Royal Family puts great focus on education in exo-politics. Knowing the history of other species is vital to understanding both foreign cultures and our own. Many cultures have long histories of generating complex and baffling religions. If any society produces a rational and demonstratable religion it becomes science. Religion can be described as the art of bafflement. It never strays far from error and confusion.

Here are your orders: create a religion for the abomination. Ensure it is based on a confusing philosophy. Do not lead them to truth or clarity. Instill the virtues of obedience, hard work, cooperation and un-inquisitiveness.

A study of ancient cultures, in this region of the galaxy, will provide excellent inspiration to you.

To Kin and Dutchess Shera

The plan so ordered is brilliant. If you cannot eliminate the sensitives you can employ them in an endeavor which is constructive to our aims. Keep me informed of your progress.

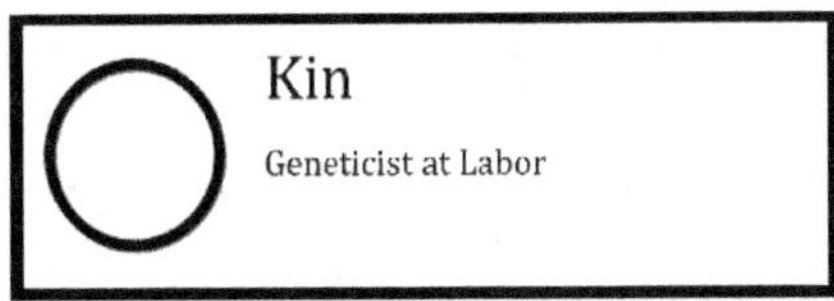

To Baron Rotha

CC: Royal Associates

I must report a failure. My Igigi and I constructed a religion. We based it on the religion of the prophet Mohetiad of the desert planet Jahshrab of the Bairainian solar system. This religion provided all the listed requirements. It emphasizes work, obedience and a very well-ordered society. The Jahshrab religion provides the foundation of a successful society on a meagre and mostly desert planet.

The Igigi appeared as angels of light. They taught the principles of the new religion. The Igigi employed a quad beam emitter. It put the abomination in a magical and receptive emotional state. The abomination seemed to fully understand and believe the new religion. At every meeting with the Igigi they beamed with love and understanding. At the end of every lesson they appeared to understand and believe without reserve.

The abominations are too chaotic, and I must add, too clever for a religion. The most intelligent were the first to break the spell of the lesson. The least intelligent never did break free. The lower third are typically the least intelligent, with some surprising exceptions.

The most dominant and influential also soon broke free. In hindsight this was inevitable. The abomination have a flighty and ever-changing mind.

No lesson can stay long in their mind. They cannot focus on anything for long.

The influential began to remember the lessons wrong. They infused the wrongly remembered lessons with their own wishes and fears. The religion quickly devolved. Dozens of sub religions emerged. Quarrels began over which sub religion was correct. Influential religion leaders convinced followers to give them gold discs so they would not have to labor.

Because of infighting and un-laboring leaders, I ordered the Igigi to return. They announced the religion had been withdrawn because of the misdeeds of the abominations. I believe that no religion will survive the chaos of their minds. I believe no religion can survive the belligerence of their interactions.

To Baron Rotha

CC: Associates

Inform your charge of the error of the experiment. The proper religion is based upon the target recipient. The Royal Family has a rich history of creating successful religions, in the ancient past of the Anunnaki. A reproduction of a distant religion from a dissimilar species is doomed to failure.

Religion must be a mirror of the desires, fears and aspirations of the target species.
Religion must incorporate elements of life as it is commonly lived.
Therefore list the primary hopes and ambitions of the abomination. List the fears and pains, as well as common experience of your abomination.

To Baron Rotha

CC: Royal Associates

I see your point. The abomination greatest hope and desire is to be dominant. The aspiration of all abomination is to be the alpha. But the alpha manifests in multiple ways.

They have a confused mind. They re-interpret the instinct of hierarchy into the drive towards kingdom. They confuse the All-man's clear pattern of animal hierarchy. They do not strive for perfect and stable order. Instead they create kingdoms of every little skill and talent.

They dominate by giving speeches and telling stories. They dominate by parenting. They dominate as teachers, preachers and professors. They become a mini-king of each conversation. They never establish a stable hierarchy for long. instead they move from mini fiefdom to fiefdom.

It worries me a little. They have the same instinctual drive to hierarchy as all mammals. They receive the drive through the All-man. They receive it as do all mammals. But the drive becomes disguised as ideas. This gives their ideas more importance than they deserve. I fear their ideas will produce much disruption.

One abomination priest made a new religion of his idea. He argued that everyone should have the same number of gold discs. This, of course, would undo all that we have accomplished. This led to a battle of ideas. The battle of ideas led to violence. The violence interrupted work. I had the new priest destroyed.

Their young men are fearless. They fear nothing except humiliation. The recklessness of their young men is a great challenge. Without intervention, many would do foolish things which lead to injury or even death. Their children have a similar naïve boldness.

They all fear violence from each other. A percentage of them always perpetrate violence. I have attempted many modifications to eliminate the violence. I can decrease overall testosterone release. But generation after generation, the percentage of violence does not vary much. Lowered testosterone only pacifies them in a general way. Pacification has an unwanted side effect. They do not work hard. The top producers are very aggressive at task. Without these aggressive workers we cannot maintain acceptable production.

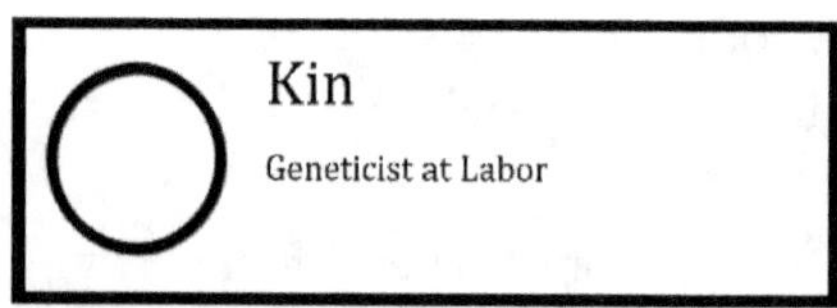

To Baron Rotha

CC: Royal Associates

Mining of gold ore commences. The Igigi and the abomination have constructed the habitations. The abomination and the Igigi have instituted agriculture. Agricultural harvests continue to improve. The population of abomination is 127,101 living. 75,794 active laborers, 40,033 laborers dedicated to agriculture etc., 35,761 laborers dedicated to mining. Our average daily mine production has not stabilized so I leave it uncalculated. We continue to solve problems of production. We continue to solve problems of all types.

To Kin and Dutchess Shera

I applaud the success of this operation. Keep me appraised of your progress.

Do you expect agriculture to continue to demand such a high number of abomination laborers?

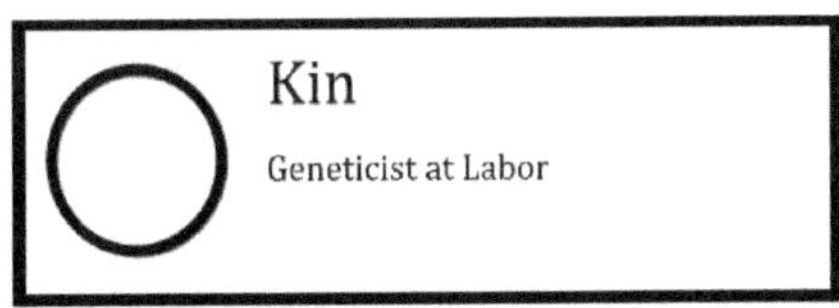

To Baron Rotha

CC: Royal Associates

I expect the labor percentage for agriculture to remain steady. If we require more labor for the mine we must increase the overall population. If we increase overall population it must include a corresponding number for agriculture, children, mothers and other support personnel.

I had intended to send the following information as a separate communication. Since the beginning of this project I have assumed all our doings are under the continual surveillance of the Saurians. Since our move to the Absutu their craft have often been visible as they observe our activities.

To Dutchess Shera

(Reserved for your eyes only)

Kin reports visible Saurian activity. Please advise.

To Baron Rotha

(Reserved for your eyes only)

The Saurians have protested all of our activities on this planet. Their protest began the first day Enkin set foot on the soil. Any escalation of Saurian activity is cause for great concern. Keep me appraised of any notable events regarding the Saurians.

To Dutchess Shera

(Reserved for your eyes only)

I was not aware our project is protested. I am not experienced in exo-politics. Please advise.

To Baron Rotha

(Reserved for your eyes only)

Exo-politics is the exclusive domain of the inner circle of the Royal Family. It does not concern you. Keep me informed of all actions and suspected actions of the Saurians or any other new arrivals.

To Kin and

CC: Dutchess Shera

Keep me informed of all actions and suspected actions of the Saurians or any other new arrivals.

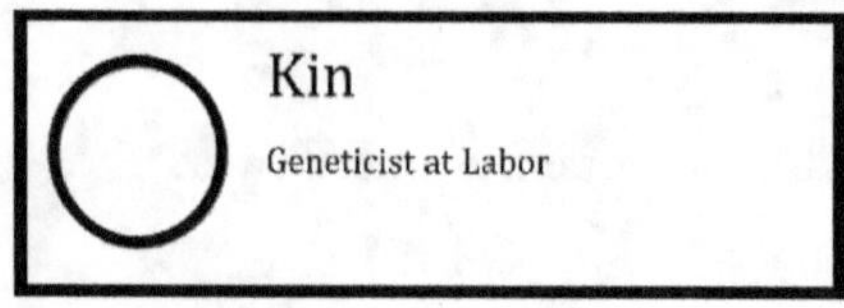

To Baron Rotha

CC: Royal Associates

Automated facility security sends automated reports on every sighting.
Automated security has sensory capabilities superior to any living observer.
I assume the correct recipients receive the reports.

To Baron Rotha

(Reserved for your eyes only)

I inform you in the strictest confidence that there has been an oversight in
the processing of security reports. The protests of the Saurians have
escalated. Your project is now a delicate exo-political issue.

To Dutchess Shera

Shall I take any additional measures?

To Baron Rotha

Keep me closely informed of progress and any changes to your project. Any expansion of the mining operation must be approved.

Additional security equipment is scheduled to be installed at your project location.

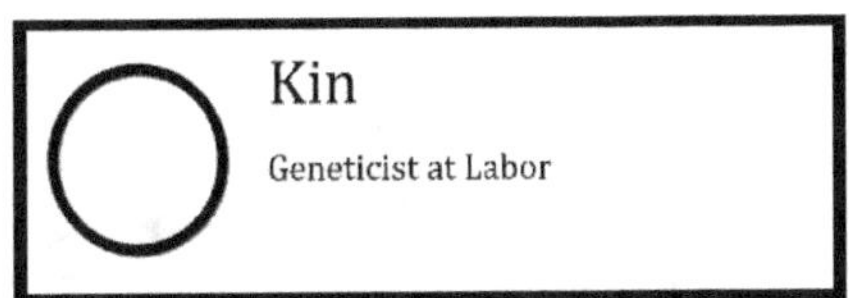

To Baron Rotha

CC: Royal Associates

We continue to follow the gold ore body downward at a steep angle. The pile of refuse rock continues to grow. An Igigi pilot commented that it is visible from the highest boundary of the troposphere.

The new security equipment has been installed. I no longer have access to the security reports. I assume this is as intended. I am content to leave the burden of security to others.

The triple grade plus ten social system continues to be productive. We recently had a noteworthy killing. An abomination, which more often falls in the bottom ten percent, killed the most productive and able leader. The three families in the challenger houses left. They have not returned. I expect they fear for their lives.

Because the killer was typically on the punishment of the ten percent, I devised a new punishment. I instructed the Igigi to remove the eye of a recently deceased abomination. I ordered them to graft it in place of the killer's nose. All abomination saw the killer with an eye where his nose used to be. Afterward the killer was destroyed.

Dutchess Shera

Royal Dutchess of Karn
Superior of the
Royal Order of Saturn

To Baron Rotha

CC: Associates

Commendation is in order for the novel and creative form of punishment/motivation.

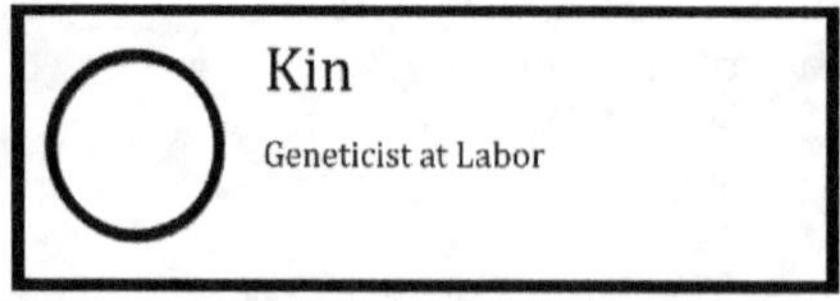

Kin

Geneticist at Labor

To Baron Rotha and Dutchess Shera

Urgent report!

As the mine reached minus eleven miles depth we encountered an existing horizontal tunnel. The tunnel contained transportation rails and other technology. A number of abomination miners performed an unauthorized exploration of the tunnel. They were killed by defense drones. I dispatched reconnaissance drones to ascertain the nature of the tunnel and to discover its owner. My reconnaissance drones were destroyed. I have halted work and withdrawn all abomination to the surface.

To Kin and Dutchess Sherra

Attach an in-depth report of events leading up to and including the confrontation.

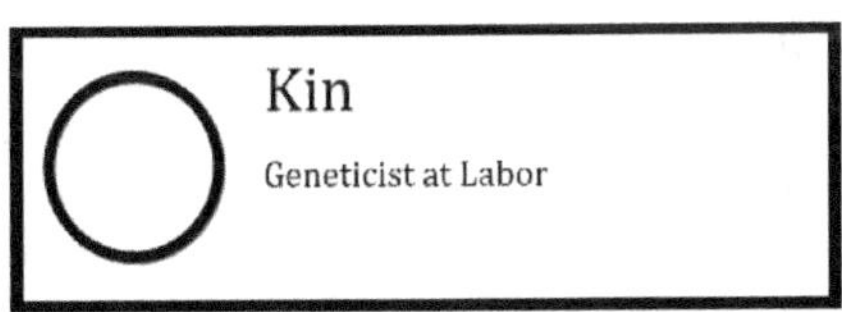

To Baron Rotha

CC: Royal Associates

Attached site report.

Site notes year plus 925

925.07.12

Daily progress: nominal, (see production statistics), no incident to report.

925.07.13

Daily progress: 56% of normal, (see production statistics), multiple incidents reported.

925.07.13

Incident report 1

Lead abomination in charge of cutting charges reports variance encountered. Mining halted until a new plan can be put in place. Reconnaissance drones dispatched. Reconnaissance drones destroyed. Abominations reported missing. Work halted. Workers withdrawn to higher level.

REPORT: Abomination in charge of cutting charges

Cutting charges detonated. Unexpected collapse of floor. Tunnel encountered. Technology encountered. Operation halted. Request for new orders.

REPORT: Abomination in charge of mine surveillance

Report of variance received. Reconnaissance drones dispatched.
Video feed recorded. Drone 01 lost contact. Drone 02 dispatched. Drone 01 video feed reviewed. Unknown drones encountered, hostile action. Drone 02 lost contact. Drone 02 video feed reviewed. Unknown drones encountered, hostile action. No further drones dispatched. Request for new orders.

REPORT: Abomination in charge of rock removal

Cutting charges detonated. Work crew moved into place to cart away blast-cut rock. Unnatural mine tunnel encountered. Four of the work crew climbed down to investigate. None returned or responded. Two of the work crew climbed down to find fellow workers. Three more investigators followed down. From a distance they observed the previous two workers disintegrated by unknown drone. The three investigators successfully fled from the drones. Remaining crew ordered to flee to higher level. Request for new orders sent.

To Dutchess Sherra

(Reserved for your eyes only)

What further actions need to be taken?

To Baron Rotha

(Reserved for your eyes only)

The Royal family is in council.

To Dutchess Sherra

(Reserved for your eyes only)

I expect we have encountered a Saurian transportation tunnel. I expect they were aware of the location of our mine activities. How great a problem is this?

To Baron Rotha

(Reserved for your eyes only)

Because their cities are underground, the Saurians have stated that digging more than 100 feet down is considered an act of extreme aggression. We have denied any mining activities.

To Dutchess Sherra

(Reserved for your eyes only)

The Saurians are known to be generally peaceful. Do they protest our attempt to preserve our planet?

To Baron Rotha

(Reserved for your eyes only)

The first rule of politics is discretion. We have not announced our project, nor have we expressed our needs. We do not announce our intentions. It would be a breach of discretion to present a weakness of our people. We do not express any deficiency of our planet. We have denied the project exists.

To Dutchess Sherra

(Reserved for your eyes only)

I have no doubt that the Saurians are fully aware of our project. Our refuse rock pile is visible from space.

To Baron Rotha

(Reserved for your eyes only)

We have maintained plausible deniability of a contested project. Leave politics to the inner family.

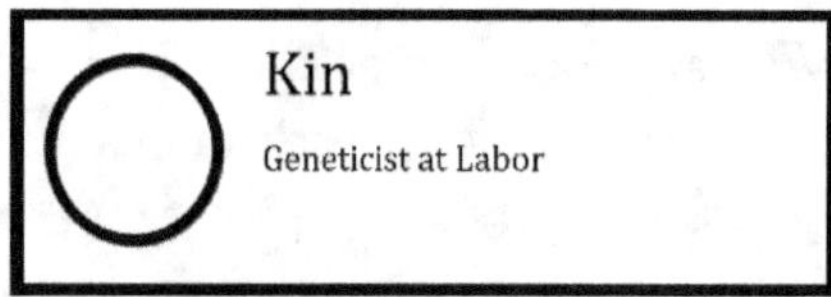

To Baron Rotha

CC: Royal Associates

Urgent report!

Violent confrontations increase in frequency among the abomination. No mining work currently proceeds. I have left the miners in their graded houses as before work ceased. The agriculture workers protest that the miners receive a gold disk reward without work.

The sides of the conflict are not clear. I can only use statistical analysis. Statistically, the lowest third of agriculture workers protests the top third of mine workers. But violence most often occurs between the lowest third of agriculture workers and the middle third of both mine and agriculture workers. Statistically the punished ten percent of mine and agriculture workers inflict the most killing and serious injury.

The top third of both mine and agriculture workers avoid conflict the most. Leaders from the middle grades of both mine and agriculture workers have organized fighting groups. Most of the violence across all groups is by young men.

I believe the only solution is to begin a new mine. Only work can return the social order to normal. The violence increases. At present I fear the loss of this project.

To Dutchess Shera and Kin

I consider a new mine the best solution. Is this acceptable to the Royal Family? Is a suitable ore body close to the existing housing and agriculture?

To Baron Rotha

CC: Associates

Deliberation is proceeding. Do not proceed without authorization.

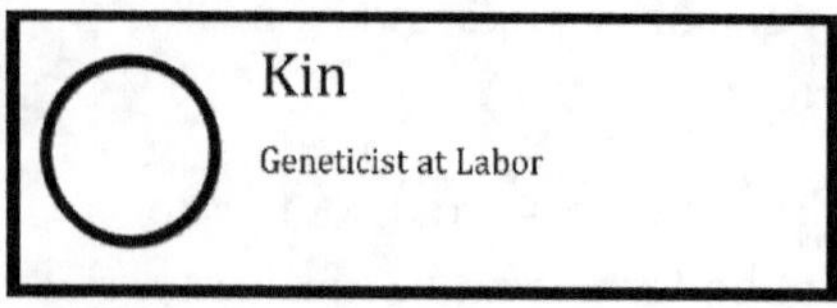

To Baron Rotha

CC: Royal Associates

A suitable ore body is workably close. I await authorization.

A small group of top third mine workers have left the habitations. They attempt to live like animals in the nearby mountains. My Igigi are fully employed attempting to limit damage and violence. Their efforts are partially effective.

To date our project has produced thirty-five percent of the gold needed to protect our planet. We have not reached the critical amount needed to create an effective shield.

To Baron Rotha

CC: Associates

Effective immediately you are authorized to begin a new mine in the proposed location. You are authorized to mine to a depth of five miles and no deeper.

To Baron Rotha

CC: Royal Associates

I proceed to mine at the approved location to a depth not to exceed five miles.

To Baron Rotha

(Reserved for your eyes only)

Saurian protests have escalated from demands to threats. As our ore carriers enter and leave the Earth's atmosphere Saurian ships fly critically close. If hostilities proceed a military commander will take my place. He will command your every resource.

To Dutchess Shera

(Reserved for your eyes only)

I am at the full command of the King and his appointed authorities. Do I need to take any precautions?

To Baron Rotha

(Reserved for your eyes only)

Ensure your shuttle is always ready for an immediate departure from Earth.

To Kin

I command you to always have your shuttle at the ready for an immediate departure from the Earth. Order the same for your Igigi.

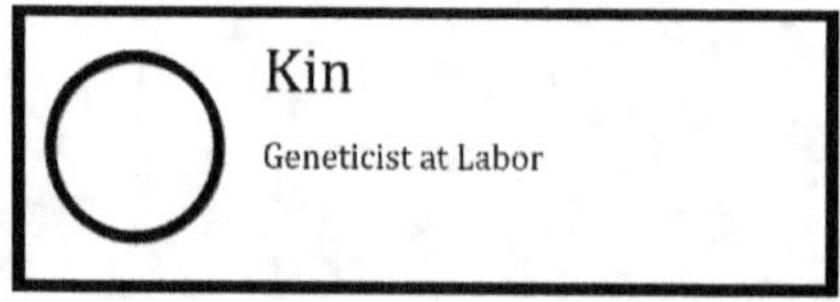

To Baron Rotha

CC: Royal Associates

Work has begun on the new mineshaft. The abomination have generally returned to peaceful productivity. I expect to have ore ready for processing by the end of the month.

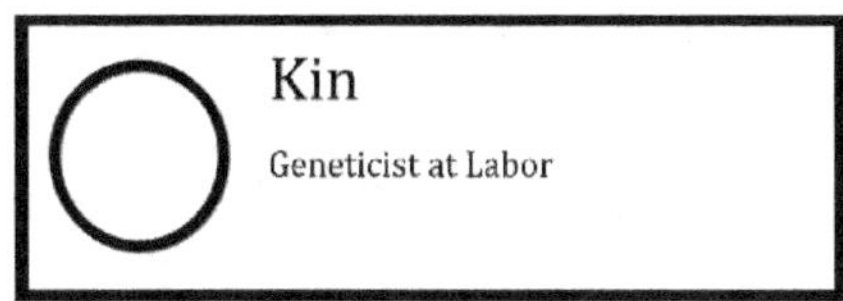

To Baron Rotha and Dutchess Shera

Urgent report!

Two disc-craft hover above the new mine at all times. The abomination are unsettled. I am also unsettled. To ensure a safe exit, I need one more standby shuttle for the Igigi.

To Kin and Dutchess Shera

I have allocated two additional shuttles for the Igigi and an additional shuttle for you. If we are ordered to depart, all shuttles are to depart simultaneously. This will impose more potential targets to any potential enemy. The chance of survival will thereby be increased.

To Baron Rotha and Kin

Conflict has escalated. Gather and evacuate all sensitive information immediately. Gather and evacuate all class A and H technology. Destroy all remaining technology. Render all structures unusable. Evacuate all our people and the Igigi as soon as these orders are complete.

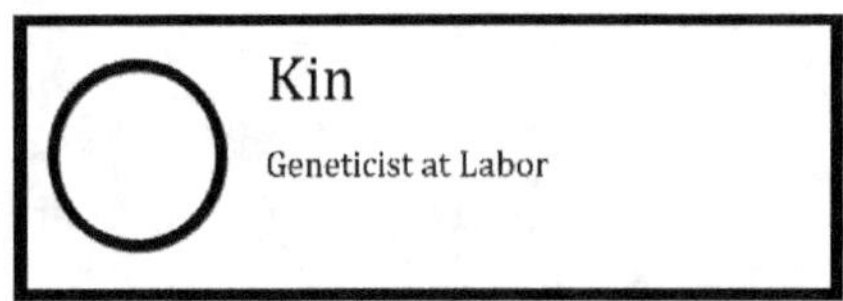

To Baron Rotha and Dutchess Shera

All required technology has been transported. All Anunnaki and Igigi structures have been destroyed except those needed for our current survival.

What is our disposition toward the abomination? Some of those which escaped to the mountains are unaccounted for. Additionally, a young male and female abomination entered the Saurian transportation tunnel. Security cameras observed them being taken prisoner by the Saurians. The uniforms of the abducting Saurians showed a double serpent. I understand this to mean they were guards of the Saurian King.

To Baron Rotha and Kin

Leave the abomination to their fate. A military escort is scheduled to accompany you and your Igigi back to our base on Mars.

To Kin

I am prepared to leave. I believed I would be the savior of our people. I expected I would return a hero. I hoped I would spend the remainder of my days in cyber-sleep as the one who shielded our planet from the roaring sun.

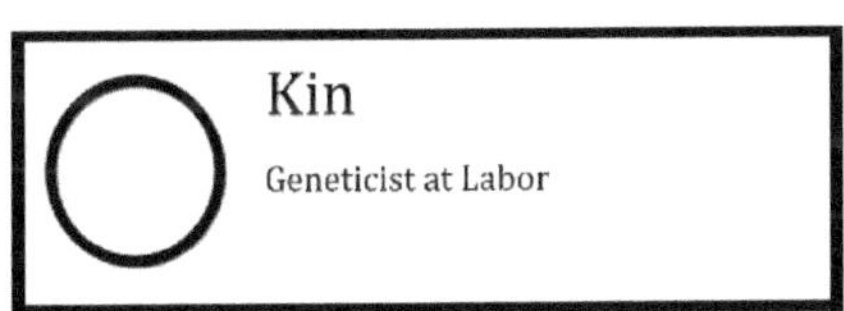

To Baron Rotha

I am ready to meet the military escort. I have left my abomination to their fate. I carry only their genes and a record of the project. I am crying Baron Rotha. My eyes will not stop. I will meet you in the mists of Saturn.

Part Two

Attack of Rotha

Interlude

We do not know of our elder siblings, the Saurians. We do not know about the first species of this solar system, the Anunnaki.
We have two neighbors within this solar system and we are not aware. Now we have new visitors within the solar system. We must become aware. We know nothing of those visiting from other solar systems.

Resource explorers have found us. Now that they have found us, we have entered into the adult world. We now play the big game. We are like an adolescent entering the *city* of the galaxy. We are no longer sheltered in solitude

Most often other species do not share our morals and values. Most often other species do not have emotions similar to ours. Even if they do, they are not always in a position to act with heart. Necessity makes every species push up against moral boundaries.

Everywhere in the galaxy, life is hungry and therefore competitive. Do not expect a benevolent species to come like a loving mother. Do not expect a great and loving species to share unlimited knowledge and power. Such do not exist.

Our visitors are highly civilized. But civilized does not necessarily mean good. Civilized does not necessarily mean friendly or helpful. Look at our own civilizations. They are full of many organized ills. We must understand that our visitors are competitors.

Part Two

Attack of Rotha

Kin, Lab notes, Personal Log, year plus 952

I have committed to keeping a personal log. I may find it useful
for future projects. It might be enlightening to posterity. It will
certainly break up the monotony of this dreary Phobos base.

We didn't make it back to Saturn. I had hoped to be put back
in cyber-sleep. My original term has only forty-eight years
remaining. I expected to refuel at Mars. I did not expect to be
escorted to a small room with no accoutrements but a bed.

I am ordered to remain in this ghostly annex wing. Rotha was
escorted to the officer's wing.

Kin, Lab notes, Personal Log, year plus 952

The young Anunnaki who delivers my meal has begun to talk
to me. I will not include his name. He is part of the research
division on the base. He also despises the restrictions inherent
on a base which is primarily military.

His ambition is to study the Saurians. Because he is young he is restricted to the study of the abomination on Earth. He believes I can give him information which will aid his ambitions. Having been a junior researcher, I know only time will give him senior responsibilities. Skill or even genius will not. I don't have the heart to tell him.

Kin, Lab notes, Personal Log, year plus 952

My young research friend has given me every detail of the fate of the abomination. He considers them a short-term experiment of little consequence. He tests me often to see if I know something about the Saurians I have not already told him.

The agriculture area has been largely abandoned because the industrial inputs from the Igigi were destroyed. A few groups maintain a part of the original plantation. Most of the abomination have dispersed. It surprises me how far they have spread geographically.

Their culture can only be described as feral. They wage a constant but unorganized war against each other. They can only maintain groups of less than fifty before they split into smaller warring factions. They have not established anything resembling a town. Their overall population has grown. This surprises me.

Kin, Lab notes, Personal Log, year plus 953

I am still confined to quarters by the military command. My young researcher still delivers the meal. He reports military operations are underway. He complains he has been denied all access to information about the Saurians. Many of his Earth surveillance drones have been commandeered by the military.

He reports some abomination groups have collected naturally occurring gold from streams. Other groups have attempted to dig caves. There may be a residual instinct remaining from over three hundred years of mining operations. I very much want to study this. But I am confined to quarters for the time being.

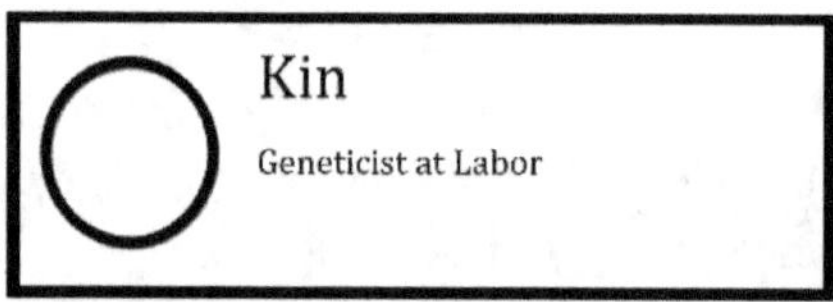

To Baron Rotha and Dutchess Sherra

I have surmised that the abomination have survived, disbursed and proliferated. I want to continue to study the abomination. I believe they may be of future importance. I am, however, confined to quarters in the Phobos facility. I request authorization to join the research team stationed here.

To Baron Rotha

(Reserved for your eyes only)

A hot war is in play. Operations are ongoing. All non-essential personnel
are confined to quarters. All transports are committed. Flights to Saturn
are highly restricted. You and your accompaniment are to remain on
Phobos base until further notice.

Inform your charge to communicate through the chain of command
only.

To Kin

Because of ongoing military operations we are confined until further
notice. Travel to Saturn is not forthcoming. Do not contact Dutchess
Shera directly.

The situation is more severe than I expected. Comfort yourself in the
knowledge that we have done all we could for the King and the
greatness of the Anunnaki people.

Kin, Lab notes, Personal Log, year plus 953

My young research assistant has a natural gift for gathering
information, even information far above his grade. He has
informed me the Saurians have destroyed every facility and
device we had left on the Earth. They also thoroughly removed

our presence from its moon. They have banned us from the planet under threat of violence.

I fear I may become much too familiar with the four walls of this room. I requested access to the hallway for the purpose of exercise and mental comfort. My request was denied.

The Office of
Baron Rotha
Lord of Annunaki genetic programs

To Dutchess Shera

I grow weary of the officers' wing of this facility. I have stopped taking dinner with the military personnel. Whenever I enter the room the conversation stops. I am eager to continue to Saturn. Can you give me a time frame to shape my expectations?

Dutchess Shera
Royal Dutchess of Karn
Superior of the
Royal Order of Saturn

To Baron Rotha

(Reserved for your eyes only)

I tell you in the strictest of confidence, the conflict is far from over. The King has decided to remind the Saurians that the Anunnaki are the oldest and dominant species in this solar system. Comfort yourself in the knowledge that you have done all you could for the King and the greatness of the Anunnaki people.

Kin, Lab notes, Personal Log, year plus 955

I have gathered more stories from the young assistant. A
number of Saurian cities have been destroyed. Apparently
sonic devices were inserted above the cities many thousands
of years ago. They drilled down at a rate of about one foot per
year. Because of their slow action they were not detected by
the Saurians. The devices produce sonic and counter sonic
vibrations. Ships landed on the ground above the cities. The
ships pulsed sonic vibrations into the rock. The buried devices
use constructive and destructive interference to align and
focus the sonic waves from the ships. The barrels became a
node in a standing wave. The nodes were spaced in order to
create a linear compressive standing wave. The Saurian cities,
located at the end of the standing wave were destroyed.

I fear my time here may be unending.

To Baron Rotha

(Reserved for your eyes only)

Keep this in your strictest confidence. The King has ordered the total
number of awake to be increased from 12% to 20%. Process is underway
to waken the additional 8% of Anunnaki from cyber-sleep.
Most of the awake will be devoted to intelligence gathering.

Do not hope for a timely return to cyber-sleep. Keep ready. You may be given a new assignment.

Kin, Lab notes, Personal Log, Kin, year plus 968

I have paced the room back and forth for months. I question if I should contact Rotha. I learned that the Saurians have modified some of the abomination. They have removed my lock on frontal cortex development. The frontal cortex lock was one of three developmental limits on intelligence. To remove this biological timer is irresponsible to an extreme degree. But if Lord Rotha investigates my source of this information I could lose my very valuable confidant.

Kin, Lab notes, Personal Log, year plus 1038

My young informant has given me a summary of the abomination social developments on Earth. The loosening of frontal cortex growth has not made the abomination wiser or less violent. But it has given the unlocked an advantage. They are becoming the dominant population. It has also given them the ability to envision and communicate complex building schemes. I was already concerned that I had allowed them too great an ability to build. Now that ability is enabled by expanded communication ability.

They do not build wisely or practically. But they have constructed complex cities and monuments. My young research assistant tells me in detail of the endless wars for dominance. The abomination have money economies. They have ever-shifting kingdoms. They continue to expand across the Earth.

The Saurians only have a three-hundred year life span. They are not looking far into the future. They have not considered the future possibilities they have enabled. I again have to question if I should communicate this to Rotha.

Kin, Lab notes, Personal Log, year plus 1045

I don't know why I am hesitant. I really must inform Dutchess Shera of these developments. I assume the royals have access to the research on the abomination. But they have proven to have the ability to ignore vital new developments.

The Saurians are now using the abomination to rebuild their cities. The Saurians have made alliance with them. All my work is being usurped by a species we are in conflict with.

Kin, Lab notes, Personal Log, year plus 1046

Now I am going to contact the royals. The Saurians have blocked all communications with our Earth surveillance. My research assistant reports they have no communication with their sensory devices.

I don't understand the technical aspects. I assumed that it was impossible for the Saurians to discover the nano-surveillance devices we use. Apparently it *is* quite possible to block communication with them. No signals are penetrating the atmosphere of Earth. We are now blind to the details of any new developments on the surface.

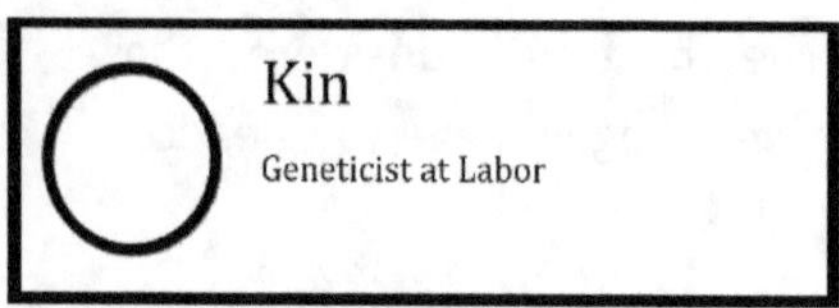

To Baron Rotha

The abomination have been genetically modified by the Saurians. A limit on their intelligence has been removed. This is contrary to the original order of their creation.

The Saurians have built alliance with the abomination. The abomination are employed on Saurian projects.

The Saurians have blocked our ability to gather further intelligence.

Have we worked so diligently to have our project repurposed? Have we committed so many resources to have our project stolen. Will we have wasted the lives of so many priests for nothing? Please forward this communication to Dutchess Shera.

To Baron Rotha

In regard to the communication from your charge.

The Royal Council is well aware of these issues.

To Kin

The Royal Council is aware of these issues.

Kin, Lab notes, Personal Log, Kin, year plus 1052

The years in this room must end. I am a corpse in a tomb. I am forgotten. They deny me the delight of cyber-sleep. They keep me awake in the desolation of four plain walls. I am not a rock to be placed and disregarded. A plan foments in my mind.

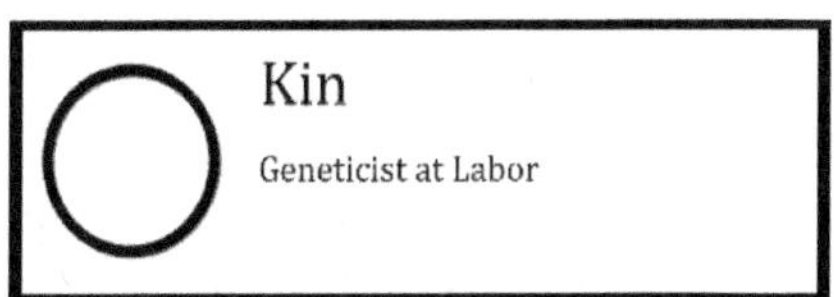

To Baron Rotha

Please forward this communication to Dutchess Sherra.

I have three desires. I will to deny the Saurians control of my creation. I will to relock the frontal cortex of the abomination. I will to recapture the loyalty of the abomination and put them to work again. We have time to complete the original mission. We have time to mine sufficient gold.

To Baron Rotha

(Reserved for your eyes only)

Regarding the communication of your subordinate.

The three goals are impudently ambitious. Your subordinate is not aware that we are in an active war with the Saurians. The Saurians have sealed access to the Earth by transport and by communication. They have destroyed any ship which approaches the Earth or its moon. They have threatened to attack our home planet if we trespass. No one wants an escalation of conflict. Our destruction of Saurian cities is hotly debated at every table.

As an aside, he has correctly stated the three elements of a reinstatement of your design.

To Kin

Your goals are correct. Because of situations beyond our control your plan cannot be accomplished. Keep yourself ready. We may be assigned a new mission.

Kin, Lab notes, Personal Log, year plus 1054

The research assistant commented on the actions of the Saurians. He relayed the common opinion of the researchers. They believe that the Saurian attacks on us are impudent, audacious and desperate. We participate in a hot war while the sun still escalates in intensity. I feel an escalating desperation in my own mind.

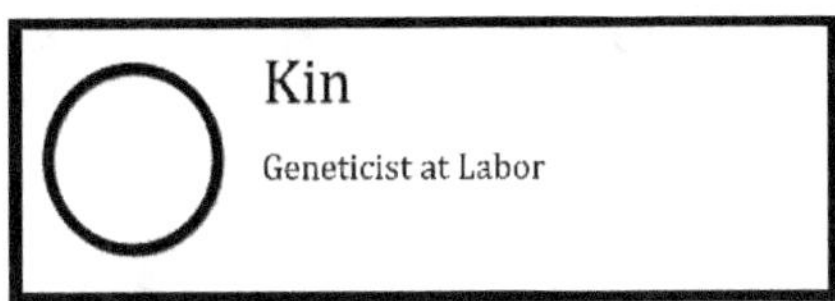

To Baron Rotha

Please forward this communication to Dutchess Sherra.

I have a design. I am first to volunteer for this audacious plan.

In order to manipulate the abomination, in order to surveil them, in order to circumnavigate the Saurian atmospheric communication block, in order to attempt to evade detection by the Saurians, In order to relock the frontal cortex of the abomination, in order to regain control of the abomination, in order to deny the Saurians use of the abominations, and in order to put the abomination to task mining sufficient gold, I propose: to secretly construct an underground facility on Earth with a genetic laboratory and surveillance capability. To staff it with myself and the one-hundred loyal Igigi heroes. And there to accomplish the design with a minimum of communication or transport from our people.

To Baron Rotha

CC: associates

Your charge's proposition was audacious indeed. Even more audacious is that the King has agreed. The King himself has set his order toward your design. You and your subordinate are called to a new program. Attached is the part of the Kings order as it pertains to you.

From the Kings hand...

...for a period of time unending until success or defeat.

That Baron Rotha and his charge, Kin, shall attend, accompanied by the loyal on-hundred Igigi heroes.

That they shall be entombed in the secret facility without communication or re-supply, unless it be initiated by military command.

That they shall recapture the loyalty and cooperation of the abomination or that the abomination should be destroyed completely.

And if possible, in full secrecy, without the knowledge of the Saurians,

that mining of gold shall recommence...

... Hear my order, so signed this day,

This is your order decreed by the King's hand.

Standby for action and further orders.

Kin, Lab notes, Personal Log, year plus 1068

I fear the King's phrase, "for a period unending until victorious or defeated." I have heard stories of missions without end. Fate-less appointees never see the light of cyber-sleep again. But even an unending assignment is superior to the four blank walls of Phobos base.

I believe I can accomplish the Kings command. I believe I can remodify the abomination. I believe we can find a way to mine gold without detection. Tomorrow we board a military transport bound for Earth. They believe they can insert us without detection.

It may be the last communication with my young informant. He described a massive mobile facility at the ready. He describes it as a very old intergalactic transport repurposed and modified.

With his talent for conversation, he gathered that the mega-pod would enter the ocean, traverse to the African continent, then slowly burrow itself into the continental rock.

All depends on remaining undetected as we enter the atmosphere. If the Saurians destroy us all my life's work will be for nought. I have a suspicion that we will enter the mega-pod soon.

To Kin

As your design has become the order of the King, I commit all to our success. I believe the military has created technology sufficient to ensure our successful insertion. Then the true test will begin.

Our first task is to reestablish communication with the standing surveillance network on the surface. There is reason to believe the Saurians have set up a communications block in the ionosphere. Therefore we should have access to our network when we are on the ground.

Our next task will be to study the present state of the abomination. We must abduct samples to assess their genetic changes. We must also understand their social development. Lastly, and most importantly, we must understand their relationship with the Saurians.

I must state in the strongest language possible, we must not be detected at any time. Our activities must be invisible to the Saurians.

At a later juncture we will discover the possibility of obtaining gold to complete our mission.

At long last we must discover how we shall take our golden prize and our lives off the Earth.

I commit all, even my very life, to the success of the Kings order and the greatness of the Anunnaki people.

Kin, Lab notes, Personal Log, year plus 1075

We have no communication with the transport which carries our pod. I can tell by our motion that we entered the oceans abruptly. Communication silence has been ordered within the mega-pod. I have heard nothing from the Igigi or from Baron

Rotha. I gather that if we made in through the atmosphere the greatest danger has been navigated.

Kin, Lab notes, Personal Log, year plus 1076

The year has been a blur of activity. (see Lab notes, Lab log) The pod had burrowed to its final destination. Communication has been established with the surveillance network. The laboratory has been set up. Parts damaged in transit have been fabricated. One Igigi died in an accident. The ninety-nine remain loyal. Rotha has communicated infrequently. He stays in the command deck. I begin my research in earnest.

To Kin

I hereby give the order to abduct a sample of abomination for genetic study. The flight-craft is to be flown by the most strict and skilled Igigi pilot. Samples are to be abducted from the target area designated. No variance to the plan is permitted. Any altercation in plan demands an abortion of the mission.

I give a standing order to any pilot in flight outside the pod: Capture is not permitted. Destroy the craft and all occupants before capture becomes possible.

Ensure these orders are known and obeyed by the Igigi. We are not an exception to this standing order. If capture is imminent we must destroy ourselves and our facility.

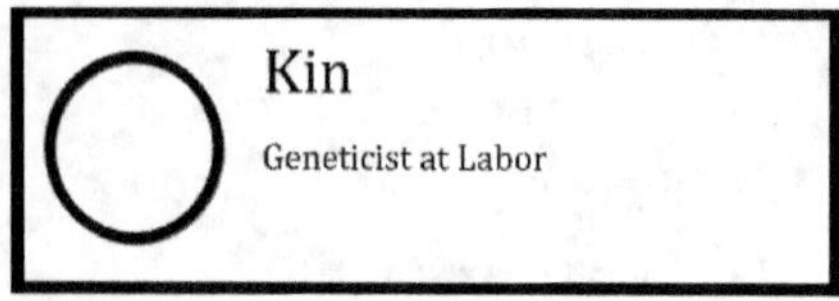

To Baron Rotha

My analysis of the abomination sample is complete. I am amazed by the number of genetic changes present. I suspect only a few of the changes are due to the actions of the Saurians. The abomination have adapted physically and neurologically. Our original concern was the frontal cortex expansion. I could create a new prototype with a re-locked frontal cortex. I have several reasons to wait.

First, we have only three priests with which to create prototypes. I wish to not be hasty as resupply may be impossible. Second, the abomination number near a million and they are spread over a very large area. A specific prototype may not be competitive. They may be destroyed by a more intelligent group. Or they might stay in a small area and not intermix with the population at large. In which case the new prototype would have no effect on the abomination population. Third, the abomination nervous system has adapted in many ways to the new expanded frontal cortex. If I limit the cortex development it may cause a host of unexpected incompatibilities with the remainder of the nervous system.

It is my opinion that we should not attempt changes to the abomination at this time. I propose to study abomination society before we revisit the issue of genetic changes.

To Kin

Your proposal is accepted. Commence study of abomination society. This study is pivotal. We must understand their society if we are to command them. I will review your Lab notes as appropriate.

Kin, Lab notes, Personal Log, year plus 1086

I have not heard from Rotha for a number of years. I don't know how he occupies his days. He has not visited the lab since it was commissioned. I have not seen another Anunnaki face since then. The Igigi report to me directly. They are a great example of cold/hard personalities. They work aggressively without emotion.

I reason to myself, my major problem is lack of communication and interaction with the abomination. I dare not risk travel to the surface. Every Igigi flight to the surface is a very great risk. Mechanical devices large enough to communicate with the abomination would be easy for the Saurians to detect. I need an emissary. I will ponder on this problem.

Kin, Lab notes, Personal Log, year plus 1087

I intend to communicate with Baron Rotha. I really don't see another option. If he rejects my proposal I don't see any other way to push the project forward.

I need a living emissary to communicate with the abomination. Initial research concludes that I can not make a successful messenger/helper prototype using existing genetic stock. At hand I have genetic material from abomination, Saurians, Igigi and myself. I will have to create another type of abomination. There is no other way.

To Baron Rotha

I need to communicate more freely with the abomination. I believe the best, even the only option, is to create a new prototype. I expect it will be profoundly different from the current abomination.

To Kin

Proceed. I will review your lab notes as appropriate.

Kin, Lab notes, Personal Log, year plus 1097

I reason out my new design. I will use Saurian genes and morphogenetics as a component. This new creation will have an appearance somewhat similar to the Saurians. I will use my own genes and morphogenetics as needed. I will use the abomination nervous system as much as possible.

The new creation will be similar to myself in size. This has several advantages. This facility has limited food production capacity. Smaller beings eat less. Also they will need to move through tunnels to reach the surface. Smaller tunnels are easier to hide and less likely to accommodate large predators. Small creatures will not be intimidating to the abomination. I reason that they will be a better messenger if they are viewed as children instead of competitors.

Experiments are underway.

Kin, Lab notes, Personal Log, year plus 1112

I understand I have created another abomination. I used two of my three priests. The results are satisfactory. I have created a being near my size. They have the ability to understand my commands. Their intelligence is more animal like than the abomination. I could not adequately block their pineal function. They can communicate with animals. They have a primitive connection to the All-man. This makes them lazy. I have been able to motivate them with gifts of food.

I intend to explain myself to Rotha after my creation proves successful. Trials are underway to train them to communicate with the abomination.

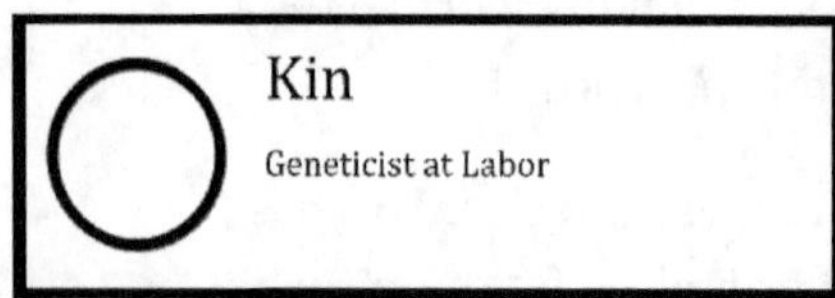

To Baron Rotha

Work proceeds toward an emissary which can communicate with the abomination. Initial tests are favorable.

Kin, Lab notes, lab log, year plus 1152

I have completed the first successful field test of the new messenger abomination. I refer to them as the Greenlings. The Greenlings look like small Saurians.

They successfully traversed the tunnels to the surface. They met abominations and communicated with them. The abominations feared their strange appearance. When the Greenlings spoke intelligibly the abominations lost their fear.

A female Greenling performed exceptionally well. In order to preserve her from the dangers of the surface I will maintain her in the lab.

Kin, Lab notes, Personal Log, year plus 1153

I begin my study of the abomination in earnest. I devote half of my time to direct observation. With the other half I program the computational intelligence to filter though the massive surveillance data. I sit inside the surveillance interface chamber and navigate. I navigate to each city. I navigate in and out of homes. I listen to the conversations of the workers. I listen to the conversations of the leadership.

Where my nano-particle network is sufficiently dense I can watch the facial expressions of the abomination. Where the network is thin I can only hear their words and know their approximate location. My overall network is spotty at best.

I need the computational intelligence to find which events are important. I have no hope of understanding the entire society without a very brief summary of all notable events. There are a million abomination and I must understand them all. I need to understand the overt and the covert. I need to understand the political and the common. I need to understand the overall developments of these new societies.

When I understand the nature of these societies we will understand how to guide them to mine gold.

Kin, Lab notes, Personal Log, year plus 1154

The Greenlings are quite limited in their ability to gather information. They can ask questions and give messages. I cannot train them to perform more complex tasks. The Greenlings are too lazy. They are not curious. They don't care about the affairs of the abomination. They can act as messengers but they are useless as spies.

Kin, Lab notes, Personal Log, year plus 1279

The abomination have spread too widely for fully effective observation. Many of their new cities and towns are not well covered by our surveillance network. Because sonic vibrations are so easy to pick up I have good audio coverage of most cities. But my visual resolution is severely limited.

I instructed the Igigi to create a drone to disburse nano-particles. I made it clear that the most vital concern is to hide our activities from the Saurians. They constructed a stealth drone. Pre-tests indicate it is suitable for the task.

Kin, Lab notes, Personal Log, year plus 1279

It seems fate is on our side. Our existing surveillance network detected Saurians at the city of Urr. This reminded me of the ever-present danger of being caught. I ordered the Igigi to add a self-destruct function to the drone. If we lose contact with the drone it will self-destruct. If capture seems eminent we can command it to destroy itself down to the last molecule.

I have no doubt that the Saurians are aware that quantum entanglement is used to gather remote sensory information. I expect they use it themselves. They may detect the drone. They may detect that someone is disbursing something. But it is not possible to trace the nano-receivers to us. And they cannot reconstruct the delivery device after it is destroyed.

Kin, Lab notes, Personal Log, year plus 1279

I oversaw the flight. The drone made successful delivery. It rained clouds of nano-receivers down on the new cities. It thickened the network on the old cities. I spread a thin network across rural habitations. When the task was complete I ordered the drone destroyed.

Now my greatest difficulty is filtering out extraneous data. I receive geop-bytes more data. I need to refine the computational intelligence to interface with the expanded data-stream.

Kin, Lab notes, Personal Log, year plus 1280

I approached the woman Greenling named Talamh. I have kept her inside the pod. She is different from her peers. I had the intent of giving her a full examination. I have become interested in Greenling reproduction. Her appearance is easier to look at than the typical frog-like skin of her kind. Her skin is smooth and a lighter color of green. She does not have the typical pattern of warts on her face. She fled at my approach. She ran like a fleeing prey. She hid herself in the lab. I did not pursue.

Kin, Lab notes, Personal Log, year plus 1285

While we have been locked in conflict with the Saurians the abomination have been reproducing. While I have been imprisoned at Phobos base they have been building. The wooden shacks of the countryside have been replaced by stone and mud brick towns. Their cultivations have spread like mold on cheese. Their towns become bulbous.

Kin, Lab notes, Personal Log, year plus 1286

I watch the abomination, feet pounding down on the hard desert ground. Under a blazing sun they toil, digging trenches, mixing mud, baking bricks then carrying the bricks to build. They are builders, ceaseless builders. At ten times my weight they lumber under the blazing sun.

Kin, Lab notes, Personal Log, year plus 1287

In the city of Urak nomadic bandits killed a farm family and drove off their flock of sheep. Long after the events I discovered that I had surveillance data of that crime. Typically the computational intelligence would ignore such a common crime. I only researched it because the event started a new kingdom.

The abomination have limited tools for creating and keeping order. They always fall back to the primitive patterns of mammalian hierarchy. They always fall to bruit force as an argument and motivation. Such was the case with this crime.

The story of the bandit attack caused outrage. No one knew the whereabouts of the perpetrators.

A strong man and his friends claimed that they could find the bandits and take revenge. They never did. But they did become the alpha group. I have seen this pattern before in abomination society. Lies lead to leadership.

Kin, Lab notes, Personal Log, year plus 1287

Talamh, the She-Greenling, remained in hiding for a full day. At days-end she made noises without provocation. This led me to her location. I interpreted this as her desire to be found. She made moves which implied that she didn't want to be captured. But her moves were weak and passive. I didn't need to taze her. It was sufficient to grab her hand firmly and escort her to the examination lab. The examination was successful. The examination included a full biological compatibility check. I report that during this procedure she was confused and resistant for the most part. As I approached completion she had a distinct change of mood. But after I completed she broke away abruptly.

Kin, Lab notes, Personal Log, year plus 1288

The abomination fear violence from each other. That is why they gather into groups for defense. Political leadership promises protection from enemies. The commoners think of the group as safety from attack. But this is only sometimes true.

The new king didn't find the bandits. But they did attack a local merchant who was notoriously unfair and deceptive. They stole some of his goods and gave it away. This increased their popularity.

Group defensive power is also used for preemptive attacks. Sometimes the preemptive attack has a justification. Sometimes it is only a thin excuse to steal from other groups.

The King's followers continued to increase in number. He had no source of money to pay or please anyone. He needed resources. He came up with an excuse to steal.

Sometimes traveling merchants are suspected of thievery. As a mule train leaves town someone may claim something is now missing. There could be a thief among the traveling merchants. Or there could be a local thief who uses the passing strangers to draw away suspicion.

Merchant mule trains always leave a trail of feces from their pack animals. This is at least one legitimate grievance.

Everyone ignored that traveling merchants buy food and lodging from the locals. The King declared one such mule train an enemy. He and his associates slaughtered the merchants. They ransacked the pack-train. It carried silk and a surprising amount of gold. This thievery financed the King's house. It also paid his chums to be permanent royal guards.

Kin, Lab notes, Personal Log, year plus 1288

The new king's misdeed did not go unchallenged. A local priest named Muuad took issue. He expressed criticism publicly. His main argument was that defensive power causes fear. When other groups fear your group they are more likely to attack.

He also argued that members inside the group would fear. This might cause them to withdraw from public life. They may also become overly compliant and unreasonably loyal. He also reasoned that a violent leadership inspires bullies and that defensive power is often abused.

The kings' chums did strut around town. Their boisterous manners intimidated the people. They took every possible advantage.

I had previously concluded that kings depend on an enemy for their own power. Without an enemy the king has little justification for existence.

I cannot know the inner thoughts of any abomination. I cannot know if an act is divisive or just unknowingly self-serving. But inevitably kings find enemies.

More than half of wars do not lead to a change of leadership on either side. The commoners are slaughtered. Royals are only imprisoned or banished. I reason that royals understand they need a permanent enemy. Therefore they spare the enemy royals.

Kin, Lab notes, Personal Log, year plus 1289

Things did not end well for the priest Muuad. His criticism reached the king. The king came up with a brilliant and devious remedy. He planted a sheep in the priest's flock. The sheep had been slyly marked with the brand of the farmer who was originally attacked. The king publicly accused the priest of trading with the bandits. No one dared complain when the priest was found stabbed to death.

There is an *implicit* justification for a king's violence against the people. The explanation is that the enemy would do worse. I think it is more realistic that the enemy would simply do the same.

Kin, Lab notes, Personal Log, year plus 1289

My latest examination of the she-Greenling went without resistance for the most part. She showed an attitude of unwillingness for the entirety of the examination. But I found that because we are similar in size we are biologically compatible in every way. My studies and experiments always include the subject of reproduction. I study the biological, psychological and social aspects of reproduction. Because the Greenlings are a similar size I can pursue more uncommon research. I believe it will be of value to Anunnaki science to understand all possible cross-species interactions.

It seems appropriate, as I have been denied the delights of cyber-sleep for much longer than my original call. Every Anunnaki agrees that the pleasures of cyber-sleep are far better than anything that can be experienced in the awake state. I feel I am due some form of compensation. I also recognize the uniqueness of my situation. I have been given untypical license. I have the opportunity to pursue experiments that no other situation would warrant.

Kin, Lab notes, Personal Log, year plus 1292

I have long suspected that the Saurians have created a secret social network. I believe it clandestinely operates inside the leadership of many cities. I suspect they sponsor operatives in all significant cities.

I have one distinct clue. I have recorded many confidential conversations between abomination leaders. They speak of information they could not have gained by themselves. The information must have come through the secret channels. I can trace ideas back through conversations to the originator. Computational intelligence has become good at organizing all conversations in a web of relationships.

My suspicion increases lately. We detected Saurians operating on the surface. But I have not yet observed any direct evidence of Saurian intervention. I have only seen them setting up a surveillance network similar to my own.

Each kingdon acts in coordination. Likely they don't know they are in coordination. They believe they are independent. I have not observed members traveling to meet. And yet they have near identical political and social goals.

Kin, Lab notes, Personal Log, year plus 1293

My surveillance network has recorded abomination rituals. Select groups dress in peculiar clothing. They chant or sing and dance into a receptive state. Then one of them takes center stage. The speaker assumes a changed voice and tells something unordinary.

These secret seances culminate in a communication received from an unseen source. I originally believed the communications to be a fraud. I believed the receiver was deceiving those assembled. I also speculated they might be expressing imagination. But these messages have a consistency. The messages of many disparate seances seem to be in coordination.

I think the Saurians use a technology unknown to me. They are known to have modified abomination genetics. It is possible they have written a specific telepathy into the genes of some bloodlines.

It is also possible that they communicate via a nano-technology. A receiver may have been implanted. I need to understand what the Saurians are doing with the abomination. I believe it is integral to human society and therefore vital to this study.

Kin, Lab notes, Personal Log, year plus 1295

Something cunning happens with abomination money. It happens too often to be coincidence. Seemingly random leaders of the money class receive key information from a séance. It leads them to riches. Then they give some of that money to a political leader. Sometimes they give it to a religious leader.

This has happened far too often to be chance. The abomination are too simple minded to coordinate this. They must be aided from an external source.

I'm trying to understand the way the abomination think and communicate. Most conversations are ordinary. Most abomination have no power in society. They have no influence. Their voice does not carry beyond a few others. But a few social networks are of great consequence.

Kin, Lab notes, Personal Log, year plus 1295

I call her to the examination room often. Sometimes I fear the activity is diverting too much of my time away from my other duties. The she-Greenling doesn't complain. She understands where the initial examination will lead to. She seems much more relaxed in the entire process from start to finish. I confess that the full biological compatibility check is the most exciting and pleasurable time of my day.

Kin, Lab notes, Personal Log, year plus 1299

I believed I had a full understanding of motivation in abomination society. Either I have encountered a new escalation or I have not fully understood.

It began with an inquiry into prostitution in the city of Aratta. This city is new and growing rapidly because of its copper mining and smelting industry.

Wood buildings are proliferating and stone structures are sometimes constructed. The mine deposit is deep. It will not quickly extinguish. Many abomination move in with the hopes of mineral riches. The farmers are the most wise. They charge much and use the high profits to expand their fields.

Prostitution has been a secretive activity everywhere. It has been condemned by law and church in nearly every city. I wondered why it had been officially sanctioned in Aratta.

Statistical investigation found the Sons of Ma had frequently used the word prostitution in private conversations. I researched related conversations from a wider area. They had secretly planned it prior to the sanctioning.

I had previously taken note of this secret sub-group. The Sons of Ma are the most prolific and influential of the secret magical fraternities. The Sons of Ma exist in every substantial city. The organization is mostly inane. But they are also involved in many mischiefs. The organization seems to attract deviants. Perhaps secrecy draws reprobates.

I devoted more time to this research than it merited. I found the local Sons of Ma had received orders from a distant leader, Jershom, in the brotherhood. The secret leadership had a plan at the ready. I could not discover the original conceiver of this plan. I only discovered Jershom who originated the specific order.

The plan worked to the leaders benefit. The miners spent their entire pay regularly. The prostitutes were intimidated into paying a keeper. The keeper was a member of the fraternity. The keeper gave a portion to the Sons. The mine owners became rich. The miners stayed distracted. The miners stayed poor and continued to need a job.

Such a complex plan is beyond the ability of the abomination. It must have a source external to their society.

Kin, Lab notes, Personal Log, year plus 1301

Now that we have been doing the examinations regularly, she takes pleasure in the full biological compatibility check. I think she looks forward to our examination as much as I do. She is playful in the act. She makes many facial gestures and sounds that express delight. I call Talamh by her name now.

Kin, Lab notes, Personal Log, year plus 1305

I ordered computational intelligence to survey the size of abomination towns and cities. Towns have grown in total population by one-hundred and forty percent since the first survey. Cities have grown by two-hundred thirty percent.

Kin, Lab notes, Personal Log, year plus 1307

When we arrived back on Earth I had several expectations. I expected to find the abomination in chaos and full of violence. I did not anticipate the complex social orders which have developed. I see coherent social structures operating everywhere.

The Saurians are known for subtlety but I can't determine how they might be shaping abomination society.

I initially expected the strongest abomination would dominate by fear and intimidation. In this I have not been disappointed. But the intimidation takes on so many new forms. I have identified four types of social empires in abomination society. These social empires dominate culture.

The first and most obvious is the political empire. It centers around a dominant leader. The leader is surrounded by an exclusive group of contenders. The hallmark of the political is luxuriant leadership and threats of violence. The leader commands the strongest gang or sometimes organized army. Some of the cities have a code or law. Others are more primitive and have only common expectations.

The second is the money empire. Nearly all the abomination cities now use money. Trade has become as important as agriculture or labor. There are a few exceptions. Distant and remote towns only trade a little. The poor and powerless are not as excited by trade and money. But the leadership of all of the four empires are avidly involved in money and trade.

I would naturally expect productivity to be the primary focus of the money empire. But the abomination are impractical and driven by a desire to dominate. Hierarchy relationships are given more attention than productivity.

A minority of workers do the majority of work. They are seldom part of the leadership. They seldom receive fair compensation. The least productive receive more than is fair. The leadership receive more than is fair.

When an abomination group reach the point of material sufficiency they do not rest and enjoy. they continue to accumulate money and belongings. They do this to impress and dominate. Any common animal would stop accumulation after the point of sufficiency. The abomination seem to have no limit.

The third empire is centered on those few with a connection to the All-man. I describe it as the religion empire. It is much less influential than the political and money empires. But it has social impact.

I have seen a repeating pattern. The truly spiritual communicate their understandings to only a few. Some of the associates become the speaker of that wisdom. The speakers then gain social influence. Because the speaker is not sensitive to the All-man they are not bound by its wisdom. The speaker tends to craft a message which brings benefit the speaker. The truly spiritual seem to avoid notoriety.

In religion the instinct to dominate expresses in subtle ways. There is a contest to see who can cohere to the admonitions of the particular prophet. There is a contest to know the dogma more completely. There is an emphasis on condemning the unfaithful. All are shows of domination.

The last empire is harder to define. I call it the empire of ideas. It is a peculiarity of the abomination. They greatly value word-based ideas. They impress and dominate each other by a display of words.
Most of their speeches are abstract to the point of nonsense. Most of their speeches are irrelevant to any real issue. They speak passionately of concepts impractically broad such as freedom and happiness. They all pretend to understand wide abstractions such as good, evil.

These abstractions can be used to categorize events in their life. But they have no use beyond broad categorization. Notwithstanding, the idea-makers take center stage. They impress and dominate with their ideas.

 Only a few of the cities produce ideas which interest me. A few of them have a rational inquiry into the nature of the physical world. Some have a systematic and rational exploration of engineering and building. Others have developed a discussion about the Saurians. But most of the abomination ideas are full of wrong assumptions and broad dream like concepts.

I might entirely dismiss the Idea that it is an empire. I might not include it as one of the empires, except I fear it may someday evolve into a legitimate science. I have a great fear of a brutal and violent species in possession of a science. Technology naturally follows from scientific understanding.

Kin, Lab notes, Personal Log, year plus 1309

My work has been disturbed many times by the woman Greenling, Talamh. When I am working alone in locked labs she sometimes crashes boxes to get my attention. She has broken necessary equipment. She is anxious until I arrive. She grabs on to me and tries to keep me from leaving. I admit I find it delightful and sweet. But I have other duties to attend.

Kin, Lab notes, Personal Log, year plus 1312

As my study of Abomination society progresses I ask what motive drives each abomination. I have analyzed the conversations surrounding King Strettus of the city of Ogg. I conclude that Intimidation is the strongest single social motivation, at least within the context of the four social empires. It is stronger than the desire for money. It is stronger than the desire for honors. It weighs heavier than the desire for love and affection. For society as a whole the instincts of friendship and family have more power. But for the decision regarding the four empires - intimidation is king.

The abomination are seldom aware of how fear of violence shapes their thinking. They grow up with it. It operates within each family. It operates within friendships It shapes their societies. Like a fish ignores water, they do not comprehend it.

Everyone who spoke with King Strettus agreed with him when they were in his presence. Many disagreed when the King was not present. Almost everyone responded differently when in the King's presence than with friends. The only possible reason is fear. The King's position, power and strength intimidate everyone.

Intimidation silences the independent thinker. The weak minded will completely change their ideas to conform. That is how they avoid the fear.

Kin, Lab notes, Personal Log, year plus 1329

In three hundred short years the abomination nations have reorganized drastically. Smaller cities have allied with one of the two preeminent cities. Two dominant nations have risen to represent the two dominant political theories.

Surveillance and reports from my Greenlings confirm, the entire abomination world takes one side or the other. I cannot understand the fervor over this slight difference in philosophies.

The Gold Preeminence philosophy holds that everyone will prosper and dominate by a rich economy. But the word economy really means those who are rich. These commoners are only a little better off than their adversaries. They believe that the rich should lead.

The Administrator Trust philosophy holds that the government is more generous than the money empire. But they do not understand, someone who gives many gifts will soon be poor. This government of distribution takes from anyone who has anything worth taking. Then they give. First the government gives to itself. Then they give to their friends. Last they give to the commoners.

The Administrator Trust philosophy is similar to gambling. Everyone believes that they will receive more than they contribute. But the administration is very expensive. The number of administrators has grown continuously. A new class of mostly useless administrators proliferates. Their jobs are a sly way the government gives.

The distribution of gifts largely misses the productive workers. Those who used to enjoy the proceeds of their labor have become the new poor. Productivity fell accordingly. The entire system therefore became poorer. Of the two philosophies the Administrator Trust is doomed to fall first.

Both nations perform the same basic social functions: civil order, military and infrastructure. Both have very similar political structures. Both rule with an intimidating police force. Both have a chief. Both have a governing body. Both use war to steal from smaller cities. Both use war to cause the people to cling together in fear of an enemy. Both have a money economy.

The commoners of both countries depend on their bosses or administrators to create order and jobs. The commoners of both countries have very little voice in the affairs of production or politics. The best members of both countries will prosper far above their peers. The commoners of both philosophies will always be subject to the laws their superiors make. Nevertheless the commoners take a side.

I wonder what would happen if the commoners had a little more intelligence and a lot more courage. The abomination are much more intelligent since the Saurians removed the frontal cortex lock. But they are still stupid and gullible.

The leaders of these oppressive organizations could not withstand even a general strike. The commoners could overthrow them if they had a reason and the courage. Abomination leadership stands on the complacency of the commoner. It is intimidation which secures this complacency.

Kin, Lab notes, Personal Log, year plus 1330

This is not the first revolt or change of king I have witnessed. But this is the largest in scope and impact. The king of Jiggre was dragged behind horses through the streets. He left a trail of blood long before he finally died. He screamed to the end. I watched as his body was dragged long after he was dead. I left the surveillance chamber feeling a little ill. He was not a terrible tyrant.

The administrator trust system died with him. The King gave gifts until there was nothing left to give. His governors took from everyone. The people became expert in hiding their wealth. The worker and the farmer became poor. The bureaucrat became most honored. Productivity lowered. When the King had nothing more to give the sycophants abandoned him. His reign ended and his enemies killed him.

The alliance of administrator trust cities fell apart. The Gold Preeminence powers swept in. They took over the crumbs of a crumbling system. They declared victory. They claimed this was proof that their philosophy was correct.

They do not understand the precariousness of their own system. They are also headed for collapse. They are not right. They are just less wrong.

I note an absurdity in some abomination groups. They have witnessed the fall of their philosophy. They still cling to it. They claim Administrator Trust is the way forward. They saw its deficiencies. But they don't understand its fall. They don't understand the system's essence or flaws. They call for its resurrection. They are a stupid species.

Kin, Lab notes, Personal Log, year plus 1331

I observe a common ritual called a bow. The strange gesture involves bending at the waist toward someone. The lowness of the bend also has meaning.

I took interest in a rebel sage named Futilose. This prominent intellectual claimed that no one should bow to another. His argument was that the gesture is derived from pack hierarchy, such as in wolves and bears. It is a form of submitting to an alpha. He held that people live by reason. Therefore animalistic gestures misrepresent civilization.

He argues, If society is based on reason then why would they suppress their strength before the royals. Why would they quiet their pride and bow before the kings?

The answer to his argument is clear. The driving dynamic in abomination society is violent intimidation not reason. The abomination society is based on their animal nature much more than reason. It is the instinct of the abomination to show mammal like hierarchy. Mammal hierarchy is based on strength and fear.

The kings are not always strong. But the guards are.

Abomination kings do not live for the greatness of their people. The kings live for their own greatness. The kings support the greatness of their allies. Every war is a lesson to the commoners. The royals rule by violence. They are strong and willing to kill.

 The royals conquer other nations by the same dynamic they conquer their own people. Every police action demonstrates the power of the leadership. Every battle against an enemy does the same.

The power of the leaders is realistically quite weak. The leadership faces limited resources. They face limited cooperation. There is a limit to what their soldiers and police are willing to do. Their laws and enforcement don't really solve many problems. The behavior of the people only change a little in response to law.

But the reason for law enforcement is not social or moral change. The reason is to rule by intimidation. When one city conquers another they do not conquer each person. They conquer the guards and the royals. They insert their king over the existing king. They merely change heads of the same system.

I did a study to gauge the influence of the philosophies of Futilose. I concluded that the commoners ignored him completely. A few of the royals discussed his ideas. My overall conclusion is that intellect has little to no influence on the behavior of the commoner.

Kin, Lab notes, Personal Log, year plus 1334

I have found myself influenced by Talamh more than I am comfortable with. She manipulates my emotions. She is extra sweet when I do as she wishes. She is bitter and unconsolable when I fail to do what she requests. She has lost all perspective of the nature of our relationship. I created her people to be messengers and emissaries. She is only kept inside the facility because I need her to continue the ongoing research in biological compatibility. Otherwise I would put her out to live with her people.

Kin, Lab notes, Personal Log, year plus 1335

The most active and largest of the secret societies is the Sons of Ma. They have an introductory program based on self-improvement and moral conduct. They give first consideration to each other in employment. They bend the law for each other. They intermarry. They enforce secrecy by shame.

The highest levels of the order have a more nefarious program. They insist on secrecy at the threat of death. They prepare the followers to take key positions of power. The network of secret relationships is impressive in size and influence. Over time they have become the power behind all major powers.

There is a mind and a will guiding them. Mostly they move toward individual riches and fame. But a subtle direction underwrites them all. I always look for a link to Saurian influence. Lately I have doubts. If it is not the Saurians, then who?

Kin, Lab notes, Personal Log, year plus 1349

Early on I constructed a three-dimensional map of population density. Overall population density has continually increased. The cities originally grew slowly. At the start, population in agricultural areas grew faster than the cities. But now a puzzling shift is occurring.

The county people are relocating in a mass migration. They leave the agricultural life of the country. They flock to the cities. I need to understand what motivates them. This is my new research priority. This migration occurs in city after city.

Kin, Lab notes, Personal Log, year plus 1350

So far I have deduced that cities provides exceptional comfort and delight. Even the brick makers work fewer hours than the farmers. The houses in the city are sturdier. The city offers a more varied diet.

The typical farmer works slowly and is very lacking in efficiency. But they work all day. The typical farmer has as many children as can survive. Every extra resource goes to expanding the family and farm. When they cultivate a new field it is passed on to the children and their grandchildren.

Why do they move to the city? First the good lands are mostly taken. When the farm children grow up there is not enough land to go around. Also the farm children have access to very few luxury items from local merchants. But these luxuries from the city give them a glimpse of a better life. They give up a delightful and personal community life. They give up a self-sufficient and independent life.

I wonder if this is the entire motivation. I think there is a hidden motive at work.

Overall I think the rural life is superior. It seems a poor trade to move to the city. One possible motivation, the city culture provides false examples of what one might achieve. Certain abomination in each field of work become famously rich. They become an example of what everyone aspires to. Almost no one can make as much money as these cheerleaders of industry. The examples of success are a deception.

They keep the pack forever chasing after a rabbit which can never be caught. This deception drives productivity and innovation. This also keeps the masses in a state of failure. They can never achieve the dream. If the people did achieve the dream they would likely stop working.

My long-term analysis is that the city system is unsustainable. New agriculture practices are at the root of it. New agriculture practices allow for a higher population. But the agriculture techniques will eventually exhaust the soil. Natural resources will eventually deplete. Then the city lifestyle will decline significantly. I feel I am still missing some part of the motivation behind these changes.

Kin, Lab notes, Personal Log, year plus 1352

Heads of commerce have become leaders in the political empires. The richest royals have become heads of commerce. The capital empire overshadows the political empire. The leadership of the two empires act as one.

This is dangerous for the stability of a society. Conflict between the four empires maintain a check and balance. When the leadership of two social empires merge it leads to conquest. Power corrupts. It causes excess ambition.

Imperial conquest is always boom followed by a bust. Over its course great empires are a net loss for society. Historically it has been the political and religious empires which merge. The merger of the political and money empires is a new development. I fear this merger more than the merger of religion and politics.

Kin, Lab notes, Personal Log, year plus 1383

I programed the computational intelligence to summarize the advancements of the religion social empire for all cities. What prompted me to search was the realization that I had not learned of anything new or remarkable about the religions of the abomination.

Computational intelligence concluded that the churches are the main source of ethical teaching. The other social empires do not have a strong and coherent view of the conduct of one's life. The other social empires have common expectations and situational rules. Only religion has a coherent view of the conduct of life.

Churches are traditional. They seldom innovate or experiment. The main lesson of the churches is that obedience and conformity are good. I wonder what abomination society would be like if the churches taught followers oppose unreasonable use of power. Likely the other empires would attack them.

I searched to understand the root power of religion. The power of religion is based on stories. Moral stories present ideas. The ideas are empowered by community peer pressure. Most of the persuasion is established in childhood, then reinforced through life.

Those whose temperament leads them to ill behavior are not much influenced by the churches, even if they attend.

Deeper research led to an unexpected discovery. Often the local parish cannot afford its church or pastor. Hidden members or the Sons of Ma sometimes channel money to successful churches. I believe they do this to propagate a common ethic. It also serves to block new or competing ethics.

Ree Tam of the city of Awan criticizes religion. He argues the commandments of the churches are impossible for the commoner to perform. This keeps the people in a constant state of failure. They can never fully succeed.

Ree Tam furthers his criticism, everyone attending church implicitly represents the message of the pastor. But few obey and perform the message well. Many sitting silently in the pews do not fully believe. And yet, their very presence gives the pastor's message credibility.

Computational intelligence was able to surveil and record the speeches of Ree Tam. What could not be ascertained is if his words had any effect. For the most part, such speeches are wasted on the abomination.

Kin, Lab notes, Personal Log, year plus 1401

I received an unexpected communication from Igigi NT0001 and FNT8494. They have never overstepped their job classification before. I was not aware that they had an opinion on any of my doings. The Igigi are known to be singularly focused on their job. Attached is their critique of my treatment of my old Greenling woman, Talamh.

From NT0001, FNT8494

It makes no sense to preserve one who is useless. It makes no sense to preserve one who is old beyond use, weak or crippled. It makes no sense to stay with one who serves you poorly while you could cling to one who supplies better. We do not understand the preservation of the Greenling woman, you have kept for these two hundred and eighty years. She can no longer please you.

Kin, Lab notes, Personal Log, year plus 1402

It makes sense to the individual commoner. If it appears they are attacked they must retaliate. They must defend themselves. Thus the commoners are pushed into war.

But the attacks are suspiciously similar across all boundaries. The reasons given for the attacks are strikingly similar across all cities. The attacks seem to be coordinated at the most opportune times. Someone is always encroaching on another's city.

 The net effect is that every group suffers oppression from some other group. All groups fear. The commoner feels weak. They become subservient to the leadership. They cling to leadership for protection. The common people are denied peace, prosperity and a happy community.

Some hidden force is greatly crippling abomination cultures. Some force is crushing their quality of life. I surveil the conversations of the powerful but I cannot pinpoint the source.

I would believe that natural ignorance and belligerence are responsible. The abomination have those qualities in abundance. I would think that the aggressive leader simply capitalizes on every possible threat. I would believe that the alphas think in terms of threat and therefore respond with an attack. But there is something else afoot.

Kin, Lab notes, Personal Log, year plus 1415

In the city of Nippur they have established public schools. The tradition grew out of a robust public forum. Even the royals participated in the forums.

They spend many hours in these schools but they are very slow to advance their knowledge. Their progress seemed to be inhibited. I discovered the oppressive dynamic. The advancement of knowledge is limited by a subtle scheme.

A culling process is built into the system. The creative are disadvantaged. The truly intuitive are ostracized. The robotic repeaters are favored. The system selects for those who put memory and conformity above intuition and truth. Advancement by testing is the way progress is stunted.

Kin, Lab notes, Personal Log, year plus 1422

The original problem was theft. I am perpetually amazed at the mischiefs of the abomination. Some bold and reckless abomination will risk all to steal gold coinage. The solution to theft is a secure building dedicated to the storage of gold.

At first the patron would pay for the security of storing their gold in such a structure. But competition ever breeds innovation. Gold keepers offered to loan out gold at interest. It was never clear exactly who's gold was being loaned. The depositing patrons only cared that their gold was available on demand.

When demand for loaned gold proved constant and an industry began. Gold storage facilities then gained more deposits when they offered patrons interest to store gold. When patrons realized they could make money by storing their gold all abomination rushed to the gold keepers.

Long after the convention of gold storage was established I made a discovery. Early on I had suspicions that the original gold theft was organized. I had long suspected that there was more theft of gold than could be reasonably accounted for. A review of surveillance data confirmed that a secret society had encouraged and supported the theft of gold. I believe they were intentionally creating a need. The thefts created a fear. It pushed gold into the hands of the keepers.

Some of the loans received from the keepers were for commerce. Some of the loans were used to build grand houses and live a richer life. The availability of loans skewed spending priorities. The availability of loans skewed what is produced. Those hungry for luxuries increased under the loan economy.

The very richest abomination had previously built fortresses to store their gold. They were immune to the shenanigans of the gold keepers. They financed themselves and their peers. They escaped the disaster this system made inevitable.

Kin, Lab notes, Personal Log, year plus 1432

I asked my special Greenling woman to gather her tribe. She walked slowly out of the pod. She returned slowly but successfully.
Her tribe followed her. They walked behind her out of respect. Talamh is the oldest among them.

I asked them about the ultimate source of the oppressive behavior in abomination culture. I asked them to search for the absolute source of the troubles of the abomination.

I have looked endlessly for a link to the Saurians. I have not found definite proof. In desperation I hypothesized the oppressive tendencies might be connected to the Earth. There might be a local feature in the Earth's mental environment.

I thought the Greenlings might have an intuition they had not divulged. They are creatures of the Earth. They have pineal function. They understand the Earth's local mind better than I.

They did a group silence. They emerged with a consensus.
The oppressive mind has its origin from the time when all
the planets were one. This is all they said.

I had to interpret it. They didn't understand it much
themselves. I assume it means some time in the distant past
when the solar system had a super-Jupiter. There is
speculation that a great Jupiter split into the present four gas-
giant planets. The greatest evidence for this is that the
elemental composition of the gas giant planets does not match
any other scheme.

We the Anunnaki consider ourselves to be the original children
of this solar system. Perhaps other species lived in this solar
system before us. Perhaps they still hold influence in the solar
system's mental environment.

Granted, the overall mental domain is non-local. But it is
understood, the local environment tunes in to certain parts of
the mental domain. It seems the original denizens of the solar
system may still echo from the past. They may echo strongest
on the Earth.

All sentient beings tend to have a desire to live forever. It has
driven the evolution of the Anunnaki since pre-history. Those
who came long before us may remain in some form. Those
who came before may still resonate. An awful, oppressive echo
from those who came before; I wish that they were silent.

Kin, Lab notes, Personal Log, year plus 1446

I continue to keep a close eye on the evolution of the gold
storage and loan business. Because gold is heavy to carry and

because it can be stolen, certain gold keepers began issuing loans in the form of a papyrus promise. Because of the convenience of the papyrus of loan the practice became common.
The inevitable result should have been clear from the outset. A portion of the abomination are liars and not worthy of trust. More often their lies go undiscovered. Their lies tend to advance them ahead of their competition. The liars prosper.

They began to issue more loan notes than gold in storage. The patrons paid little attention. Partially because they are not privy to the bookkeeping of the keepers. Also because they only care that they receive their gold when needed. Lastly because the abomination seek wealth long after their needs are met.

Within fifty years most every gold storer issued much more in papyrus note than in reserve. The short-term result was a great furry of commerce. The cities appeared to prosper. But hidden dynamics soon showed their face.

Back when gold coin was traded directly the equivalence of work and gold was generally even. Work value was easy to assess. There was a general social equality. People of greater productivity and greater status were recognized with higher earnings. But the scale of inequality was relatively small. Several factors changed this equilibrium.

Because money became more plentiful people used less discretion in their purchases. They allowed more of their income to go toward unworthy purchases. These indiscretions were accumulative.

People of little merit gained ground. Liars and cheaters gained ground. The frivolous and stupid gained ground. Simple, honest and hardworking people lost ground.

Notes of loan are more abstract. Notes are more plentiful. The cultures became richer in general. Those who are easily satisfied settled for less. Those who are more greedy fought for more. Those who are more dishonest obtained more. Those who are more robotic in their work habits collected more. Those who are lazy gained less. Those who focused on non-economic activities gained less. Those who are more creative collected less.

 No society can long endure such a system.

Those who gained more became the ruling class.

It was predictable that the new leaders would create empires of business. It was inevitable the empires of business would dominate governance. War would inevitably follow the need for resources. The business empires would influence governance to fight for natural and labor resources.

It was equally predictable that resistance leaders would arise to capitalize on the indignation of those the system dis-favored. Unending social unrest was the result. Revolution was the inevitable end.

Kin, Lab notes, Personal Log, year plus 1465

The mega businesses, with interchangeable leaders, now dominate commerce. They operate in all cities. They spread like mold on bread. They make competition impossible. There is a myth that mega businesses are more efficient. This is false. The mega businesses are less efficient. They prosper by two schemes. First, they are willing to ensnare the simple worker for slave wages. Second, they begin with a great reservoir of capital. They undercut the competition. The capital subsidizes their losses. When they drive the competition out of business they recoup their losses.

 The middle-class declines. The upper class have been persuaded and coopted. The poor are enslaved. The useless are kept alive to demonstrate that the system is benevolent. The system is not, but it appears to be.

Support for the useless people acts as a reason to increase taxes. Taxes keep a wide gap between the untouchably rich and the masses. Taxes prevent exponential growth of investments. Taxes keep the successful from crossing the gap protecting the very rich. Thereby the very rich grow their wealth faster.

The mega businesses monopolies may appear to pay taxes. But they covertly receive at least an equivalent in government assistance. No one can compete against the monopolies. The monopolies push the cities into slavery. Shop keepers, tinkerers and cobblers are pushed out of business and into servitude.

Kin, Lab notes, Personal Log, year plus 1471

After three-hundred and eleven years Talamh has died. She became old and weak. When she became so weak she could no longer care for herself I had the Igigi destroy her. I feel a distinct longing for her company.

I don't have a vivid memory of my life in cyber-sleep. I have little memory of my youth before I was allowed to enter cyber-sleep. The she-Greenling, Talamh, was the most sweet experience in the centuries I have been awakened.

Kin, Lab notes, Personal Log, year plus 1476

I found an oppressive pattern in the agricultural area of Bregda. The environment is perfect for the cultivation of wheat. Instead tobacco and sugar are grown. I had assumed that market forces dictated what is grown. This was not the case.

A local crop buyer became preeminent because he paid a slightly higher price for crops. He paid even higher prices for sugar and tobacco. Further investigation revealed he sold the crops at a loss. I could not understand how he could continue to operate at a loss.

I set the computational intelligence to wider search parameters. It took the computational intelligence an unusually long time to form an answer. I took note because of this sixty nano-second processing lag. The program sifted through all relevant sensory data eight-million times. Eventually it discovered the Sons of Ma spoke in a code language. They used words in a manner contrary to their accepted meaning.

I have given computational intelligence the idle task of reanalyzing all conversations in light of the new trick we have discovered. The abomination are becoming too clever.

The loss in profit was partially offset by high profits he charged for seed and farming implements. He received these things for a discount from a distant benefactor. I also found this distant benefactor provided supplementary coin. These additional investments lead to a local monopoly.

I suspect that the overall plan is to create addiction. Both sugar and tobacco are addictive to the abomination. I can only hypothesize why they would do this. It could be that addiction prepares the public to be ruled. A bodily compulsion sets a pattern known as 'que and obedience'. A physical addiction is an analog to being ruled by reward and the denial of reward. Such a plan is far too insightful and devious to be of abomination origin.

Kin, Lab notes, Personal Log, year plus 1489

I don't know why I gave them wings. I don't entirely understand how I gave them wings. It seemed a fateful turn of the genes. I found it necessary to create a new abomination. I call them Pixzye and they all have wings.

I tried to coax the most beautiful of the Pixzye to my office. I judged her as the most suitable for my research. She flew up to land on a structural beam, out of my reach. But she didn't hide like the Greenling. She just perched there and watched me. We looked at each other for a long time. Finally I abandoned the pursuit.

Kin, Lab notes, Personal Log, year plus 1493

No one can truly control the many conversations taking place in a city. The powerful exert a great effort to try. The leaders strive to create the foundational impressions of the common mind. The leaders broadcast the root assumptions the commoners will carry for life. Only a few of the commoners dare to contradict such official ideas.

A prominent Duke in the city of Sheer hired philosophers. He paid certain people who frequent the forums. He instructed them to advocate his philosophy. He befriended the town criers. He treated them like friends and made sure they understood his ideas. Statistically his plan was successful. Computational intelligence was able to detect a change in the ideas prevalent in the city.

Political leadership employs another devious device. They break into two groups. There appears to be an argument between two antagonists. But neither party argues against the power of leadership. They only debate who should wield the power. No one thinks to ask if the power should exist at all.

I have closely observed the subtle response of commoners to the speeches of their leaders. Most think nothing and automatically agree. Some seem to have an intuitive disagreement but they accept the ideas anyway. A few have an intuitive disagreement and can't disregard it. But they keep silent. Only a very few will voice a contrary opinion.

Kin, Lab notes, Personal Log, year plus 1492

The examination was significantly different than the examinations with the she-Greenling. The Greenlings are a coarse and earthy species. The Pixzye are soft and extremely gentle. They are not fragile or weak. They carry their strength with a soft and perfect control.

I finally found my selected Pixzye. She was unaware. I took her wrist. She bowed her head in submission. I could tell by her disposition that she would not fly away. She did not resist. But she did not go volitionally. She complied with all initial procedures without complaint or agreement. A few of the tests are uncomfortable. She took them gracefully. After the initial procedures I disrobed her. She covered herself with her hands. Her embarrassment was clear.

The Pixzye are a beautiful species. I can not control every outcome of genetic engineering. I engineer for many characteristics. I can only estimate how they will mix and express. I confess I did not intend for them to be such a handsome species. Fate always has a hand in creation.

It was necessary to pry her hands away from her embarrassment. It was not necessary to confine her on a restraining table. She submitted to every part of my examination. But the full biological compatibility check proceeded in an unexpected manner.

The Greenling was animal like during the act. The Greenling developed a habit of wrestling and wreathing until I reached completion. With the she-Pixzye the act is energetic but subtle. It has a feeling of light and airiness. When I neared completion I experienced a sense of her willfulness. It felt like she was urging me on. I cannot put into words the spirit or mood of her personality.

After completion I felt a strange emotion. It was a blend of embarrassment and regret. I have never experienced such an emotion. I hypothesized I had allowed the Pixzye too much pineal development. I believe she was transmitting her emotions to my mind.

Kin, Lab notes, Personal Log, year plus 1492

Computational intelligence alerted me to a new development. I think the program has become obsessively focused. It is excessively engaged in discovering subtle oppressions.

Food amount and quality is a most impactful oppression. Food strengthens or weakens the body, it enlightens or dulls the mind, it invigorates or makes one sluggish. Too much or too little food has a great impact on attention. The wrong type and balance of food has a great impact on productiveness.

A certain diet has become common in all large cities. This diet energizes the body but oppresses the mind. The diet is prevalent because of its low price. The price is artificially low. It is subsidized by the controllers of the economy. What they lose by subsidizing this food is regained by the slave labor of a stupefied population. The chiefs of the economy do not allow their own families to consume the oppressive foods.

Kin, Lab notes, Personal Log, year plus 1492

I have been exceptionally busy with the abomination study. I had intend to examine the Pixzye weekly. Several weeks have passed. I found the she-Pixzye alone and in a peculiar mood. I have not encountered such a mood among the Anunnaki. I describe it as a light sorrow mixed with a longing, such as missing someone, and also a crying, but not actively crying. I immediately felt a desire to comfort her. I was unsure of how to proceed. If she was an Anunnaki I would give her a gift. In cyber-sleep I would create a world element to delight her.

I reached out my hand to touch her. She recoiled from my reach. After a moments repose I held out both hands in conciliation. She placed her hands in mine. Our size is comparable but her hands are thinner and much more dainty. She bowed her head in surrender. A certain feeling arose between us. It felt like warm light. It had an ethereal quality. When the feeling reached its zenith I led her to the lab. I could feel a certain reluctance in her. But she went along.

As I performed the preliminaries I felt a sense of togetherness. I am not accustomed to any of the feelings she projects. She endured the initial procedures. When we came to the full biological compatibility check she changed mood abruptly. Her energy increased markedly. I could not tell if she was antagonistic to the procedures or not. I laid her down and disrobed her. She didn't resist.

The she-Greenling sometimes resisted at the start. The she-Pixzye was more cooperative this time than our first. The experience was as intense as cyber-sleep. Perhaps I have been away from cyber-sleep too long. I can't imagine anything being more intense or fulfilling. When I approached completion she projected a wish that it not be over. Afterward a feeling of overflowing light and happy warmth seemed to fill the lab. I lost understanding of where I was and what I was doing. It took a long time to regain my orientation.

Kin, Lab notes, Personal Log, year plus 1498

Reputation is made or broken by stories. The reputation of a species as a whole is a permanent tenant of each individual mind. Many assumptions are made based on reputation.

An audience uses stories to create imaginations. These imaginations stand where there is no real experience to draw upon. Often times the imaginations stand even when it contradicts experience.

The Pauzi have proliferated lately. They started in the city of Zabala. They began their tradition at the same time the Zabalians built their first three story stone buildings. A city with three story structures is considered cosmopolitan.

Now the Pauzi have spread to most every large city. Their tradition is to spread gossip about everyone and everything. They establish themselves in a city with a legitimate job. They typically become the town criers for the city royals. They spread the decrees of the leadership. They call the hour if the city does not have a bell. They offer their services cheaply. But most of what they do is to spread awful rumors.

I have assembled some tactics of their smear campaign. The subject of most of their gossip is Far away cities. Because the cities are distant there is less chance to discover their deceptions and exaggerations.

The far away others are presented as monstrous. Other leaders are presented as corrupt. The far away business people are said to steal ideas and steal customers. The distant educated are foolish. The distant religions are full of primitive superstitions.

The worst current events are represented as status quo. Even the worst deeds of history are presented as normal in these distant lands. The ill events are presented without any context which might explain them.

The Pauzi have a distinct and dark power over the people.

The story of the *bad others* builds group coherence. It creates a cause to build castle walls, metaphorically if not literally. It causes a group to cling together for defense.

When the species as a whole is taken to be a monster the individual will withhold from contributing. If the species is taken to be benevolent the individual will participate in a heartfelt way.

A vile world view is oppressive because it shapes expectation. Nestled in my surveillance pod I have watched abomination children after hearing such stories. I have seen them look at strangers in a new and fearful way. I have zoomed in and out. I have scrutinized their faces. I have even gained a feeling for what they feel.

When the world is a fearful place there is little place for goodwill and friendship. One effect of this alienation is unwillingness to meet new people. The result is loneliness and keeping to one's social sphere.

It benefits the leadership when the individual fears and withholds their contribution. The oppressed individual is still driven by necessity. They will go along with the activities of the society. They will be subject to it. They will not express outward. They will not make their mark on society.

It is true the abomination are a violent and chaotic as a species. But a bitter and threatening world view increases violence.

What would cause the Pauzi to spread such rumors? Are they doing the will of a secret organization? The pattern is uniform from city to city. Why do the abomination allow it? Do they understand the effect of such a world-view?

It is possible some form of entity hides in the Earths mental environment. The oppression has a high degree of intent and organization. I believe the force should be classified as an entity or a group of entities, an egregore!

Kin, Lab notes, Personal Log, year plus 1499

I have studied the religious leader Shamruew, of the city of Urr. He advocates the idea of self-annihilation or self-erasure. This religious leader argues that the mortal self is unimportant. He teaches that an imaginary and out of reach celestial being is the point and purpose of life. The main point of his sermons is that the listeners should make themselves as nothing. They should erase themselves.

There is a subtle implication in his speeches. If the listener is nothing, it is still important that they do as this leader instructs. They may be instructed that they are nothing. But they are still important enough to be commanded to obey. If every individual was truly insignificant it would not matter what they did or thought.

A person is not really able to annihilate themselves except for suicide. So a living person cannot be erased. Lacking self importance an individual is available for another to command. This is a clever form of oppression. Shamruew enjoys fame and monetary support from his adherents.

Any creature with a direct connection to the All-man would naturally put the self first and others in their proper relation. A strongly connected creature would identify the self as that which receives the greatest prize – experience. They would therefore put the self first. But the abomination do not have such a connection.

Kin, Lab notes, Personal Log, year plus 1502

Most species have a sense of the self-evidence of things. Other species would not resort to speculating about their situation in terms of word-based ideas. They would simply know it. A few abomination can know in a direct manner. Even for the adept it requires a disciplined effort at meditation.

Imagination is a reservoir of mental energy. Imagination is mental energy pooled inside the individual mind of each abomination. I modified them so they cannot transmit their emotions or visions outward.

Other species create thought-forms and project them into the mental environment. Other species project thought-forms outward and thereby release the energy. Thought-forms become part of the local mental environment. Thought-forms become part of the group-mind of the pack, troop or herd. Thought-forms become part of the group-mind of the species. Thought-forms become part of the common instinct of the species. But the abomination hold it inside.

Other species unload such a burden of conscious energy. The abomination hold the charge. In some abomination this mental charge becomes as strong as in our priests. But the abomination cannot release it. They cannot direct it. Forgetting is the only relief from their mental charge. Most of the forgetting takes place in dreaming.

The reservoir of conscious energy is the root of their fascination with word ideas. It excites them. When the abomination hurl words at each other they are projecting a shadow of mental energy.

A few of them can transform the reservoir into various forms of art.

I confess I don't fully understand the creature I created.

Kin, Lab notes, Personal Log, year plus 1503

I continue my search for the sources of hidden influence. I know the abomination gain insight that is beyond the limitations of their simple mind. I cannot see into their mind, not even with brain scans. Their minds receive a burst of... I don't have a word for it. It is not knowledge. It is not learning. I see its effect in their artists. Something comes to them. It is not directly from the origin-mind. If it were I would recognize it.

We the Anunnaki can trace the history of our knowledge. We know where our knowledge comes from. We recognize what part is from the all-man and what part is learned from other species. The knowledge of the abomination is nebulous and chaotic. I tried to build a history of it. I always reach a wall of mystery.

Sometimes I hear the abomination speak of strange nonsensical concepts. They speak of imagination or epiphany. They say an idea came to them. They cannot say exactly where it came from.

If they cannot connect directly to the pineal, if they cannot know the origin-mind directly, if they cannot know directly through the all-man, then they are receiving something - from somewhere that I am not aware of.

Kin, Lab notes, Personal Log, year plus 1512

I am observing a series of revolutions in many cities. The death and destruction is considerable. Many buildings have been set afire. Many murders have been committed. Many looters have taken advantage of the chaos.

The abomination commoners typically focus and fuss over small amounts of money. The leaders typically focus and fuss over small quotas of productivity and profit. Now they all destroy so much more than the trifles they have gained.

They make one stride forward and slip back three. They could have easily made a more equitable system. They could have preserved the peace. But that was never the real objective. The abomination seek to dominate. That is why they are so willing to destroy so much of their cities.

Leaders within the Sons of Ma have prepared for this inevitability. They have a plan at the ready. They have already made relations with mercenary groups. For now, they wait. I expect them to make a grab for power when the fighting parties have exhausted themselves.

Kin, Lab notes, Personal Log, year plus 1513

I kept my schedule to examine the she-Pixzye. I expected no resistance. I was surprised to find her unwilling, even mildly combative. She exuded a cold fire against me. Her condemnation was palpable. When I touched her to guide her she shook her arm away. She followed where I led but she walked with a stomp. When she submitted to the initial procedures she acted as if she were alone even though I was beside her. I did not continue to the full biological compatibility check. I led her to her quarters and opened the door for her to go in. Before she went inside she showed an emotion which I could not interpret. It seemed she had regret and missed me although I had not yet gone. When her door closed I stood and pondered. I lost count of time.

Kin, Lab notes, Personal Log, year plus 1515

Ritual sacrifice is a way of identifying sociopaths. Some members of the Sons of Ma demonstrate an absence of conscience. They show a willingness to follow that which violates all moral compass. Sociopaths and slave minded followers will reveal themselves by a willingness to participate in bloody sacrifice.

The Sons of Ma initiate potential leaders into their highest ranks by ritual human sacrifice. This is used as blackmail. This weeds out the heartful. It ensures the candidate will do anything they are instructed. By this scheme the perfect servant is groomed to lead society. First they must show they will violate their heart, soul and all social expectations.

Kin, Lab notes, Personal Log, year plus 1522

Since most of the revolts have been rectified a new tone of leadership has emerged. Hyper-leadership now flourishes in most cities. The abomination leadership has become stronger, more necessary, more powerful, more justified and deserving of more resources.

Hyper-leadership rests upon a dubious morality. They form an official definition of what is proper and good. Hyper-leadership hinges on the people accepting an official definition of what is acceptable and unacceptable. Things frowned upon have become legal crusades.

Many natural abomination behaviors are problematic, such as drinking and loose sex. Many common behaviors often bring trouble. They might possibly be harmful. But the case is seldom certain.

Statistically, such behaviors, in aggregate, may be a detriment to society. But individually they are often benign. Drinking, drugs, sex and other expressions of joviality are the most common examples. A less strict and less focused part of society are the typical offenders.

The behaviors cannot be stopped completely. In fact they cannot even be reduced by a third. They cannot even be eliminated completely from the ranks of the leadership.

Yet leadership declares these actions as wrong, harmful, immoral and therefore unlawful. The leadership persecutes the wrongful. The leadership punishes the wrongful. The leadership stands for the elimination of the wrongful behaviors.

Because the behavior is natural and inevitable the prosecutors will have an endless supply of violators. The punishing system will have an endless supply of victims. They will have an endless supply of criminals, sinners, enemies of the state and enemies of religion. They will have and unending need for prisons and police and soldiers and counselors and priests and teachers.

Because what they fight against is natural and inevitable they will never solve the problem. They take strong action. They expend significant resources. They trample many people underfoot. They only make small gains.

They hail their small victories as success. They lie about the progress of their programs. But the problem remains. And so does the need for their power.

The abomination are stupid. The common people will never understand the game played against them.

The leaders are aggressive and assertive. The leaders focus on hierarchy and action. The lieders may have a little understandings of the dynamics behind their power. But I see little evidence of the leaders being contemplative. The abomination leaders are not philosophers, they are dominators. Few of them really understand what they are doing.

Kin, Lab notes, Personal Log, year plus 1530

Our military transport delivered supplies and further communications. Attached is a communication from Tar.

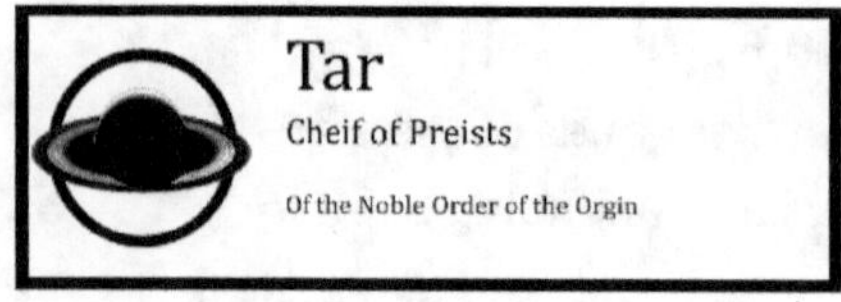

To Kin

I congratulate you on the progress of your project. I trust your success will save our planet from much destruction. I write you preemptively. In case you have a cause for further experimentation.

It is like the wars of old. An army of priests have already been sent. An army of priests have fallen for the cause. Too few remain. My abodes are empty. My halls are silent. The libraries are full of ghosts. No more priests will be sent.

Kin, Lab notes, Personal Log, year plus 1531

I have long noted a particular mysteriousness in the Greenlings. I saw a subtle similarity between the Greenlings and some of the priests. I made an intuitive gamble. I attempted to use a Greenling to enliven an experiment. I used a simple monkey as a test subject. I created the monkey from a genetic template. There is no way to bring life to them without a spark from the All-man.

I employed a quad-beam emitter. I used it to modulate a Greenling into a meditative state. I had hoped to induce a state similar to that achieved by the priests in meditation. No Anunnaki has ever enlivened sentient life without a priest. I am the first to initiate life by alternate methods. The Greenlings can be used instead of priests.

The power of the Greenlings may be due to the priest I used to enliven them. He was the most magical and mysterious of all the priests. I observed his priestly practice. It was different. He had developed his own meditations. He seemed to commune with the Earth rather than the All-man. When he took his life to transfer his spark, his body flew away from its spot. The Greenling prototype convulsed. The priests body flew from the foot of the new Greenling and hit the wall. I had never seen that before.

Kin, Lab notes, Personal Log, year plus 1533

The Igigi were busy with technical projects. I decided to destroy my latest abomination prototype myself. I had allowed the new prototype of abomination to procreate. Their offspring proved to have no advantage over previous models. This was my first time personally destroying a creation. I had always ordered the Igigi to do it.

I led the family of abomination into the destruction box. They clung close together. I observed them through the glass wall. As I prepared the apparatus the abomination appeared to become aware of their fate. I do not know how simple creatures could understand the apparatus and its function. The children clung close to their mother. As I moved to actuate the machine the father rushed aggressively toward the glass wall. At the same time the mother and children clung more tightly together.

At the moment of destruction, it seemed to me, for a very brief moment, a surge of very warm mental phenomena burst from the mother and children. It felt like a primal emotion had divided in two. I had a momentary understanding. It was as if something had split into the rage of the father and the warmth of the mother and children. I have nothing similar to compare it to. It seemed to pass through my heart. It seemed to pass through my eyes and make them sting. The destruction was successful.

At first I wondered if the event had caused me harm. I have since recovered.

Kin, Lab notes, Personal Log, year plus 1533.2

I have not been resting well. I have neglected eating sufficiently. My thoughts have been unfocused and irrational. I feel I have lost something when nothing has been lost. I have an irrational feeling the Igigi know something is wrong with me. I will take a break from my tasks.

Kin, Lab notes, Personal Log, year plus 1533.5

I have given her a name based on the name her people gave her, Airly. The Pixzye speak a language they invented themselves. It is a combination of languages. They learned language from abomination, Igigi and myself. They also use words reflecting what animals have communicated to them. Because I left their pineal intact, they understand the simple thoughts of animals. They spend the majority of their time in the surface forests. This saves space and resources in the pod.

I have surveilled them interacting with the forest creatures. They build friendship and alliance with any animal which is capable of such a relationship. I have given them a very light work-load so they have time to develop as a society.

Airly has access to all parts of the facility other than security level H. She searches and finds me. She waits quietly as I work. She can wait all day if I am absorbed in a task. As soon as I appear free she jumps on me playfully.

Kin, Lab notes, Personal Log, year plus 1542

I used my last special Greenling to create a new batch of Greenlings. My intention was to replenish my stock so I can continue to create new protypes. I must report a failure. After ten attempts I concluded that the new Greenling can not be used to spark life.

The progeny of the special priest were unique. I had always assumed I could make more. If I had realized my supplies were so limited I would have been more selective in which prototypes I attempted. I am consoled that I was able to create the Pixzye. They are my greatest success as a geneticist.

Kin, Lab notes, Personal Log, year plus 1544

I have been examining my Pixzye almost daily. I confess I typically skip the preliminaries. I reason that I have gathered enough data. She seems to not like the preliminaries. She wants the same experience as I. She goes directly for the full biological compatibility check. She craves it. I confess I do too.

It is difficult to describe the feeling of her contact. She feels light, as if she weighed nothing. Her mass is three-quarters of mine but she feels like a feather. Her touch is feathery and gentle. When she is on top of me she cannot hide her true weight. At all other times she gives the impression of a wisp of wind.

Kin, Lab notes, Personal Log, year plus 1549

King Gotchu led the city of Urr to become the strongest and most modern city. I asked computational intelligence to give me the most pivotal events leading to his success. It noted this speech.

I watched this speech personally. My surveillance dust was dense enough to record it in detail. This speech outlines his philosophy of oppressive rule. He has somehow gathered together all possible crafty and oppressive strategies.

King Gotchu's speech to his cabinet.

Esteemed brothers and comrades. I have invited you to know my philosophy and my plan. I give it to you in the strictest of confidence. With your life as payment you keep it within this group.

My six step plan is already succeeding. It has already been proven. Now I expand it. Now I intensify it. It is power. If you follow my plan you will share in my power. If you ignore me you shall be subject under it.

It begins with six clear steps:

1. Amass wealth

2. Control the public conversations

3. Demoralize and destroy competing social structures

4. Establish secret societies

5. Oppress the whole. Promote the few

6. Own and control the economy

1. Amass wealth

Money is a powerful motivation. In time it can become the preeminent motive of the culture. From the very beginning amass wealth. In the later stage own the money supply. The approach used matters little, weather by a kingly chairman, president or a central bank.

Own the major industries. The rulers must own the industries jointly, they will then operate as a hidden monopoly. The cost of living will be established. The direction of technology will be determined. The dominant way of life will be set.

Own and control the major investment platforms. We can tax the investor in many subtle and clever ways, such as stimulated market crashes. The rise and fall of stock value can be manipulated. The common investor needs to see the market as the best and easiest gains for their excess capital. They will not share proportionally to the economy's real growth.

Create a few "cheerleaders" as examples of investor success. The followers will dream that they can accomplish the same. Of course very few will enjoy such success.

Take only a little money directly through government taxation.
Tax much more indirectly. I will instruct you in this. Taxes keep
compound wealth from realizing. Taxes keep the somewhat
wealthy from competing against our leadership.

Remember that money is relative. It only matters that we have
much more at our disposal. With greater leverage we will buy
their sons as soldiers and workers. And we will enjoy their
daughters as whores.

2. Control the public conversation

To lead we must control the minds of the people. Therefore
build an industry of mass communication and teaching. Make
it inexpensive to the commoner and free to the poor. Make it
appealing to the masses. Incentivize creators, actors, writers
and producers.
motivate them all with a dream. Pay the select best an
extraordinary amount. The followers will dream that they
might one day make such unattainable money. Praise the
select best with special fans. We will pay and guide the fans.
They will create fame. Make the followers believe they might
one day receive the same inordinate honors.

By this we will control the content of the public dialogue. It is
our message which will be understood.

3. Demoralize and destroy competing social structures

The main point here is to weaken trust and goodwill. To weaken
self-trust is to limit how much love one can give. To weaken
trust in others is to limit what love one can receive.

Love is the fountain of creation. We will not stand for the wretched commoners to command such a power. We will do the creating. They will follow.

Destroy trust. Destroy trust in government. Destroy trust in business leadership. Destroy trust in economic self betterment. Destroy trust in religion. Destroy trust in the civility of the common person. Destroy trust in international relationships. Destroy all trust and replace it with fear.

Destroy hope. Let them chase after out icons. Secretly they know they cannot compete. They may dream they will one day grow strong enough. But today they know that our champions surpass them.

Burden the people with an onslaught of suffering. Fill them to capacity. Keep them filled to capacity.

When drama is ubiquitous they will be desensitized. Desensitize the people so they can be acted upon without revolt.

Destroy traditions which we cannot appropriate. Destroy them by derision. Let our honored speakers disparage the tradition we oppress.

Destroy institutions we cannot control. The wild institution is an enemy of the kingdom. Even if it is full of benefit, it must be destroyed. We will control all institutions and traditions.

4. Establish and maintain secret societies

Partition off the new appointment from society. Also alienate him from the fraternity he joins. Destroy all trust by demanding secrecy. When the neophyte agrees to keep his vows a secret he intuitively knows that greater secrets are kept from him. He will not trust the secret society. He believes the commoner should not trust him because he keeps secrets. But he will pursue the fraternity to learn power.

Destroy solidarity with the city and community. When we demand that fraternity brethren be given priority - the member becomes separated from the city and the community. They are no longer members of the common. But they cannot trust the secret society because it keeps secrets from them. Thereby they are trapped. They must be made to put the secret organization above city, community, law and religion.

Organize a secret chain of communication from the highest leadership to the lowest spy, even to the lowest neophyte. Create a tangle of relationships within the order. Within the organization we can find a person for every job, no matter how dark the work. Word will find its way up and down the tangle. Secret jobs will be assigned. Guilt will not find its way back up to us.

5. Oppress the whole. Promote the few

Again I tell you the main task is to weaken trust and goodwill.

Create heroes which put the people to shame. They will believe that they could achieve as much. Because they cannot, they will be ashamed. To be ashamed is to be subservient.

Use law excessively to make the common people afraid. Give some reprieve to those of the secret organizations.

Create and support religions of submission, guilt and resistance to new ideas.

Create and support an education which portrays the self as nothing, accidental, animalistic and therefore contemptable.

When the common people see no hope they will collapse into hedonism. The money economy can provide for their desires. We will have tight control of the common wage or benefit. This will prevent the commoners from destroying themselves with excessive hedonism.

The few we promote will be dis-illusioned of these burdens. They will be supported and somewhat welcomed among the ruling class.

6. Own and control the economy

When all the aforementioned elements are created and maintained to a high degree total control will be certain. Economics is the keystone. The money system will be owned.

 The religions will be outlets of our philosophies. The religions will be aligned with our laws. The learned will be taught from our books. The political leaders will be selected by our choice. They will be at our call. The military leadership will be populated from our secret societies. We shall pay them all. We shall own the society. We shall own the world.

We shall declare each city as industrial or agrarian. We shall declare each city technocratic or primitive. We shall declare a people fit for a limited democracy or for tyranny.

We shall lead them to a perfected world. We shall ultimately promote the fit to breed and the unfit to dwindle in number. Ultimately the worthy shall be our allies. We shall be masters of the rest.

This is my plan. I have prepared a place for you at my table. I have work for you to accomplish. Expect my orders soon. Fulfill your part and you shall share in the glory. It has already been established. Tonight I decree it!

Note: I must note that after King Gotchu died his city lost preeminence. Empires are always boom and bust. Societies based on a charismatic leader die soon after the leader. The abomination do not have long lives. They cannot see the inevitable collapse of the empires they fight so hard to build.

Kin, Lab notes, Personal Log, year plus 1550

I consider my study to be complete. I have a sufficient understanding of the state of abomination culture. Although I will continue observation and analysis I can make solid conclusions.

We can trust the abomination to continue being chaotic, aggressive and ever evolving. Certain social aspects are reliable:
The bulk of abomination will submit to outrageous leadership. Leadership will seek domination, wealth and preeminence.

Gold and other monies are the most powerful sources of influence. The secret fraternities are the most manipulatable thread in the web of abomination culture. The fraternities can be used to great effect. But it may take many years to enact such control.

The religion and idea social empires are the weakest. They can only be used toward long-term shaping of social ideals.

The political and money social empires are the strongest.

The most sure way to motivate the abomination is to pay workers.

Kin, Lab notes, Personal Log, year plus 1552

I confess I have dropped all pretense of study in the full biological compatibility check. Airly is by my side most every hour. She only leaves if she has meals with her family, when they visit the facility. She shares my bed. I no longer consider her a creation or test subject.

Airly is at my arm all day. She is by my side day and night. My days are warm because she is here. My time flows like water because she is here. When she sees my eyes she is all. I cannot remember a time before her or imagine a future without her. I apprehend all that I feel for her. But I cannot comprehend it.

Part Three

Success of Rotha

Interlude

Resource explorers have found us. Our solar system resides along a navigable star-way. We have been discovered many times in the distant past. But now we sustain a large and technological population. Now we are ripe for inter-species trade.

Relations between species are inherently political. Relations between species are of lasting consequence. The destiny of a planet can change with one exo-relationship.

The wise remain hidden. The wise only reveal themselves when necessity demands. The foolish inform all the galaxy of their resources. The foolish broadcast their strengths and their weakness. The foolish will soon be dominated. The foolish will be milked like cattle, sheared like sheep.

It is naive and child-like to expect the galaxy to be beneficent. The clever will pretend to be friends. The clever will create dependency within our society. Dependency inevitably leads to domination.

We are not the only denizen on this much coveted planet. We share consequences with others. This record of events acts as a most basic primer on exo-politics. We must quickly become wise.

Part Three

Success of Rotha

To Baron Rotha.

Military Command surveillance has completed a biological survey of Earth. They have detected two species of interest. They request information regarding the species pictured in the attached arial photos.

To Dutchess Shera

I have not received briefings regarding new arrivals or unknown species.
The photos have limited detail. On request, I will forward these to Kin
for comment.

To Baron Rotha

Do not forward photos. Military Command has decided on a course of
action. Standby for further orders.

To Baron Rotha

The habitations of the species in question have been identified. A
military drone will dispatch to prepare samples for collection. Order
your Igigi to receive the bodies and deliver them to the lab for full
analysis.

To Kin and Dutchess Shera

See previous conversation. Order the Igigi to receive the samples. Prepare to analyze subjects upon delivery. Prepare a comprehensive report of your findings.

Kin, Lab notes, Personal Log, year plus 1553

I cannot understand why the military would take interest in the Greenlings and the Pixzye. It seems a waste of time and effort.

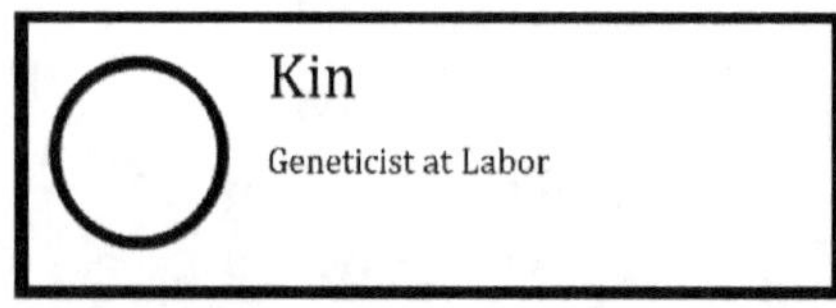

To Baron Rotha

(**For Your Eyes Only**).

Uncatalogued species are irrelevant to the mission. I have ongoing work. This task is a distraction from more relevant tasks. Can you delay their mission?

To Kin

(Reserved for your eyes only)

Most of the newly awakened Anunnaki are engaged in intelligence gathering. Let them wet their curiosity. It is of little cost to us. Send a reply confirming your cooperation, CC Shera.

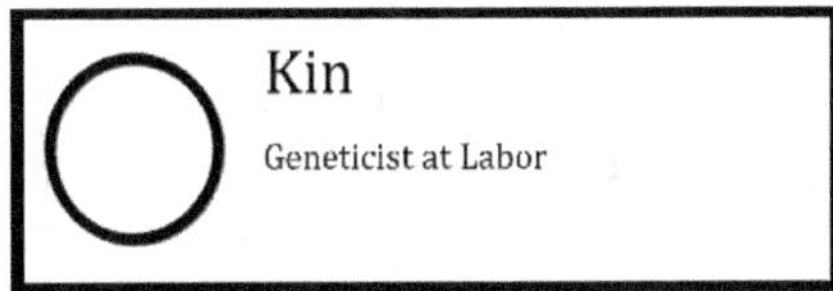

To Baron Rotha

CC: Royal Associates

I am fully engaged in preparations to receive and analyze the bodies.

Kin, Lab notes, Personal Log, year plus 1553

She needs her family to be happy. I need to warn the Pixzye, but I have no regular communication with them on the surface. I occasionally am able to surveille them flittering about the surface forests. I have very poor coverage of the forest.

I would think that Rotha would at least know that I created the Greenlings. But now that I review my personal logs, I think he may not. regardless, I need the Greenlings as couriers. They don't return to the pod regularly. I need to warn them all and recall them to the pod.

Kin, Lab notes, Personal Log, year plus 1553

I debated the issue within myself all day. But from the start I knew there is no alternative. My love must travel to the surface. I can not keep her safe and let her family and kind die. She would not survive such a shock. She could not endure such aloneness without her kind.

I sent her to warn the Greenlings and all her kind. I gave her a deadline. She must return by sundown. I do not know when the slaughter drone will be dispatched. I do not know if it is already hunting. I told her to only travel under cover of the forest. I told her to travel in creeks and gullies. I explained that a hunting machine will kill her the instant she is seen. I told her she must explain quickly to her people. I ordered her sternly, if they do not believe then leave them to their fate.

She departed an hour ago. I fear for her already.

Kin, Lab notes, Personal Log, year plus 1553

I can not see where the Pixzye are. I have full view of all entrance tunnels to the pod. I wait vigilantly.

Kin, Lab notes, Personal Log, year plus 1553

Pixzye approach the pod. I have programed security to admit them all. I have detected no sign of my Airly.

Kin, Lab notes, Personal Log, year plus 1553

Eighty percent of the Pixzye have made it to the pod. The Greenlings move slower. They have begun to descend into the entry tunnels. Sundown approaches. I have no sign of Airly.

Kin, Lab notes, Personal Log, year plus 1553

The sun has set. I was distracted by the flood of creatures entering the pod. I had to reassure them and find a place for them. I have no sign of Airly.

To Kin

Military operations are complete. Prepare the lab to receive biological samples.

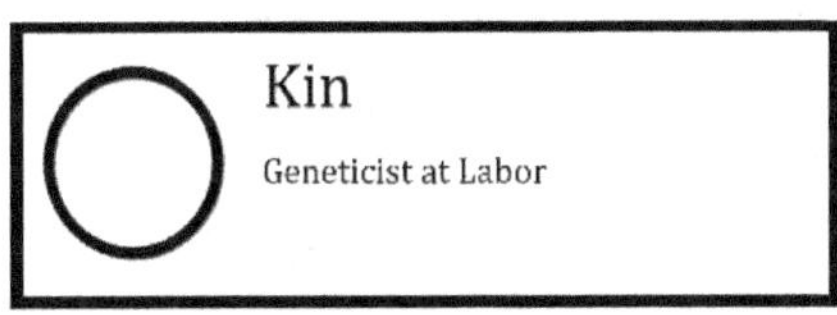

To Baron Rotha

What samples?

To Kin

The military drone has retrieved samples of the unknown species.
Complete the analysis with all due haste.

Kin, Lab notes, Personal Log, year plus 1553

The drone entered the landing bay. I watched from the control
room. It opened belly hatches and unceremoniously dumped
twelve corpses on the floor. Then it left. I waited in fear. I
dared not look. Finally I went to look for my love. I saw nine
Greenlings and three Pixzye. My love was not among them.
She is still on the surface.

Kin, Lab notes, Personal Log, year plus 1553

My Pixzye returned three days after she departed. She was
dirty and ragged. She watched two of her kind killed by the
slaughter drone. She hid inside the hollow of a dead tree. She
feared the entire time. She only ventured out when she feared
starvation. Her kind needs to eat frequently. She was too
depleted to fly. She dragged herself through the forest until

she found ripe berries. I give all my attention to her
rejuvenation.

Kin, Lab notes, Personal Log, year plus 1553

My people killed her people. I dissected and analyzed their
corps. I can't tell her. But she can tell I am greatly disturbed.
She offers me her warmth in return for my participation in
their slaughter. My people contend with the Saurians and it is
the most gentle and beautiful creatures that are slaughtered.
The military slaughtered them out of curiosity.

Airly tried to join me in lab number eleven. She has been in that
lab by my side many times. I had to push her out. She grabbed
me and tried to stay. She craved my company after her ordeal. I
had to push her out of the lab and close the door. I couldn't tell
her why. I had to hide what was inside.

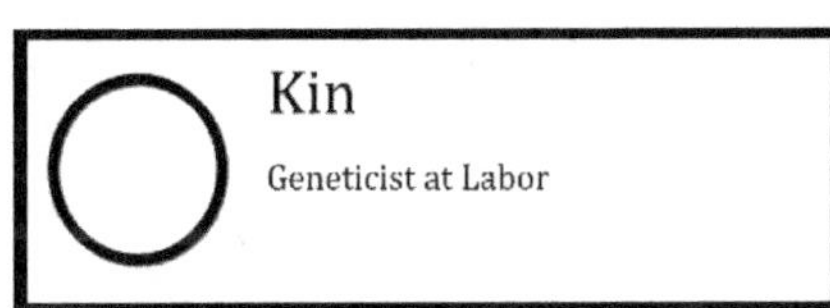

To Baron Rotha

I have performed an analysis of the corps delivered. My overall
conclusion is that they are creatures from Earth. They belong to the
biology of the Earth. We can rule out the possibility that they are new
arrivals. Both species are primitive and appear to be untechnological.
One hypothesis is that they are species thought to be extinct.

I have attached a holography of their DNA. I believe it offers the most detailed record for future study. I confess that the file is gigantic and difficult to navigate. But it offers the most detail.

Feel free to contact me for further information.

Kin, Lab notes, Personal Log, year plus 1553

The mega-pod was not designed for the current population. The Greenlings and Pixzye have reproduced to a significant population. I do not have enough food production capacity. They fill rooms not designed for habitation. The Greenlings tried to build a village out of lab equipment. They use devices of the highest technology as building materials.

This situation is not sustainable. I will ask Rotha if the slaughter drone is still active. I need to return them to the surface.

Kin, Lab notes, Personal Log, year plus 1553

The Greenlings are more robust. I sent them out first. Rotha reports the slaughter drone is not presently active. The word "presently" scares me. The memory of the slaughter drone scares the Greenlings. They have not ventured much beyond the caves. I fear that trauma has laid the foundation for a new instinct. The Greenlings seem all too willing to live in caves permanently. The surface is a much nicer environment.

Kin, Lab notes, Personal Log, year plus 1554

I instructed my Greenlings to ask the abomination if they know of the location of gold. Their answer brought me the realization that I have made a great oversight. The Greenlings don't know what gold is. They don't understand that gold is the only reason we are here. Gold is even the reason I created the Greenlings. I have since instructed them all in gold and gold ore.

Shortly thereafter nearly every Greenling brought me a sample of rock with gold nodules covering the surface. They have been living in underground caves since the attack of the drone. Their main cave system is in a conglomerate rock. Ancient geologic processes brought gold infused water up in contact with the conglomerate rock. The conglomerate is coated with gold specks and visible gold crystals. The samples they provided are uniquely rich. I will task them to explore. They have implanted trackers. Their exploration of the cave systems will give me an idea of the extent of the gold bearing rock.

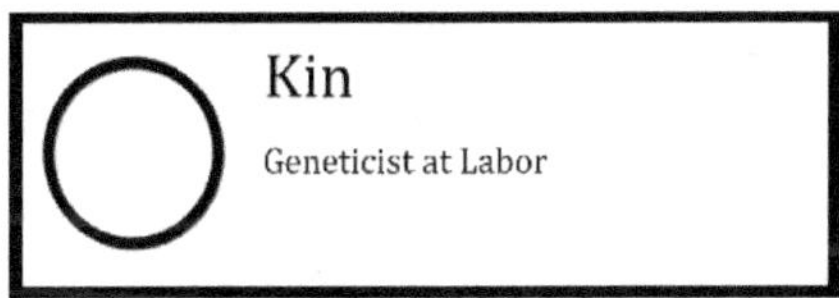

Kin

Geneticist at Labor

To Baron Rotha

I have discovered a massive deposit of gold. The ore body is richer and larger than I could have hoped for. All of our needs can be achieved. But the ore is widely dispersed. There is no possible way to mine and process the ore by conventional technology. First, we would be detected by the Saurians. Second, the pod does not have the industrial capability. We are not able to fabricate the machinery needed to mine at this scale.

I am at an impasse. Do you have any resources of which I am not aware?

To Kin

I am delighted by your report. Our success is assured. We are at the very edge of saving our planet. We will devise a method.

The next scheduled communication and resupply is in twenty-five years. Devise a method by that time. Perform experiments in your lab to prove the concept. I trust we have all available knowledge in our databases.

Congratulations and keep me closely apprised of your progress.

To Kin

I have prepared an order.

Whereas we have discovered a suitable gold ore body. But we cannot mine it by conventional methods.

Therefore I order:

Research the nature and extent of the ore body.

Research all knowledge of possible ore extraction methods.

Inventory all industrial resources in the pod.

Discover or invent a method of ore extraction which meets the following criteria:

I must not be detectable to the Saurians. Therefore it must be a primitive technology.

Because raw ore requires too much transportation we must process the ore ourselves to a reasonable purity.

The ore must be delivered no later than three-hundred years hence, as we are already fifty years into the start of the nova cycle.

After our success I will coordinate transportation of the gold off planet.

Hear my order, signed this day, Baron Rotha

Lord of Anunnaki Genetic Programs.

To Baron Rotha

I receive your order and consent. Work is underway to complete the order.

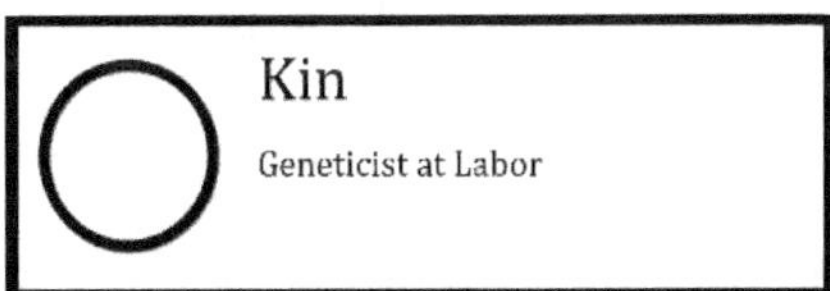

To Baron Rotha

My research concludes that solution mining is the only possible option. Gold can be dissolved from the surface of ore with the appropriate chemicals. We do not possess these chemicals. We cannot produce these chemicals. They must be found in nature. If the gold can be dissolved from the host rock it can be collected. I have already identified an impervious strata of slate below the ore body. It is fortunate that the impervious layer is not too deep. I must then devise a method to collect the gold from the slate bed. I have some hope that we can accomplish this mission.

To Kin

Your report brings a brilliant sunrise to my heart. I can see the accomplishment of all our hopes and ambitions. Keep me closely informed of all the pivotal events of your progress.

Kin, Lab notes, Personal Log, year plus 1554

I dispatched all my Greenlings to collect rocks from the countryside. They are very strong. They are similar in size to me. They can carry a rock sample which I can't lift. I instructed them to bring any rock which is jagged. A rounded rock has been eroded by water transportation. I need to map where all local rocks come from.

Kin, Lab notes, Personal Log, year plus 1554

The pile of rocks the Greenlings bring is out of control. I have
ordered them to stop collecting samples. They never were
great at obeying orders. The Igigi spend all their shift
cataloging the incoming rocks. I need to find a place outside
the pod to dispose of the cataloged rocks.

Kin, Lab notes, Personal Log, year plus 1554

My map of rock origins indicates that certain nearby strata are
rich in cyanide. Another area is rich in phosphate. I am aware
that cyanide solutions have been used to dissolve gold from
host rock. My problem is transportation. I do not have the
means to mine, transport or mix a cyanide solution.

Kin, Lab notes, Personal Log, year plus 1555

I have been thinking like a lab chemist. It occurred to me that I
need to think like a force of nature. Over time a river can
dissolve and transport cyanide and other chemicals. The
conglomerate is very porous. A lake above the strata will
readily seep into the conglomerate. This brings the question,
how do I divert local rivers to the appropriate locations?
Certainly excavation machines are not the answer. The
Saurians would detect it.

Kin, Lab notes, Personal Log, year plus 1555

My calculations are rough but conclusive. Farm fields above the highlands will leach cyanide into the aquifer. If the inflow is sufficient the aquifer will overflow from the base of the foothills in the form of springs. The cyanide solution is weak. But over sufficient time it will be effective.

Sugarcane is the crop which requires the most water. No farmer would attempt it in this environment. I have observed that the abomination will do anything if the price is right.

Kin, Lab notes, Personal Log, year plus 1557

Sheeray, my most reliable Greenling, has established contact with a leader within the Sons of Ma. The Greenling gives a small gift of gold at every visit. I have learned to keep the reward small and frequent. Through Sheeray I have promised the leader a very large reward if this task is completed. I have not specified the reward. I find that imagination is more compelling than an exact number.

Kin, Lab notes, Personal Log, year plus 1567

Ten years in and the abomination leader has not succeeded in leading farmers to grow Sugarcane. The abomination farmers know it is foolish from an agricultural perspective. I have promised generous compensation. No one has been persuaded. I suspect the leader is keeping part of the gold I intended as an incentive to the farmers. I need another leader for this project.

Kin, Lab notes, Personal Log, year plus 1568

The preacher Joezhet has accomplished in one year what the Sons of Ma could not in ten. I have only provided enough gold for the basic needs of the project. I have not offered generous compensation to Joezhet or his followers. My Igigi, disguised as an angel of light, appeared to Joezhet. They put him in a receptive and enlightened state with the quad-beam emitter. The Igigi said glorious things and promised all good in the afterlife. I have only promised the followers they will meet the same angel, one day.

The followers of Joezhet toil with amazing diligence. The leader of the Sons of Ma has proved to be useful after all. I ordered him to pay the farmers an exceptionally high price for the sugarcane. I also had my Greenling threaten him. I promised to turn him into a Greenling if he exceeded the portion of gold I allotted him.

Kin, Lab notes, Personal Log, year plus 1572

The plan is working. The fields soak up water like a sponge. The sugarcane grows poorly, but it grows. The leader of the Sons of Ma pays the agreed price. The aquifer shows the first signs of overflowing. I will order the Igigi to dispatch a drone to test the concentration of cyanide in the spring water.

Kin, Lab notes, Personal Log, year plus 1579

The water tests sufficient. The cyanide level is less than I had hoped, but sufficient. The phosphate level is fully saturated. I have created a workable aqueous solution. But only if I can drain it to the lowlands before it finds its way into the wrong aquifers.

Kin, Lab notes, Personal Log, year plus 1582

I have not succeeded in convincing the followers of Joezhet to dig a canal. They are farmers. They can be led to farm for a cause. They could not be led to dig all day, even for a great reward. I need a new plan.

Kin, Lab notes, Personal Log, year plus 1583

I have concluded that only a king could command a work force large enough to dig a canal. My problem is that there is no good reason to dig a canal from the foothills to the lowland plain. There is no agricultural advantage. There is no reason whatsoever. I am at an impasse. I will reach out to Rotha.

To Baron Rotha

My plan is stopped by one small impossibility. I made the abomination to farm the highlands. The agricultural irrigation saturated the cyanide rich strata. The aquifer seeped out into the foothills.

I have devised a workable solution to leach mine the underground conglomerate. I trust it will leach gold from the conglomerate. But I need the cyanide solution to pool above the conglomerate. I need the solution water to move from the highland foothills to the lowlands.

I cannot convince any abomination to dig a canal from the foothills to the lowlands. I have offered an excessive reward. The abomination will not take the challenge.

I expect that only a king could command such a massive workforce. But I have no reasons to offer them. It makes no sense for anyone to dig such a canal. In the view of the abomination it brings water from nowhere to nowhere.

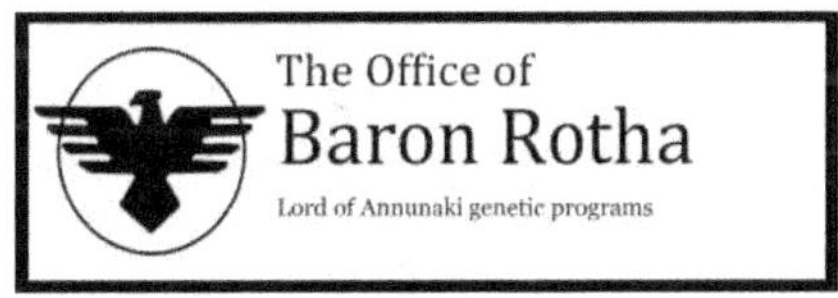

To Kin

A king will commission such a project for defense of the kingdom. Convince the King it is necessary to defend against an enemy. Create the enemy. Then the King will do as your agent suggests. Supply the King's treasury generously. No abomination king will refuse to exercise power, even if the task is foolish.

Kin, Lab notes, Personal Log, year plus 1584

I have spent a year preparing a relationship with the King of Genera? My favorite Greenling can now use the quad-beam emitter. Sheeray is becoming too old to travel endlessly to the surface. But he has no replacement. My best Greenling has become too familiar with the abomination and their cities. I surveille him on his journeys. He is not secretive enough. He is observed too many times. I expect the abomination who see him tell everyone they know. The tale will spread of a small green creature that walks like an abomination and has skin like a frog.

I reprimand him upon every return for his carelessness. But I must also reward him for his efforts. I prepare an exclusive meal. He will obey my command as long as I provide his special dish as reward.

Kin, Lab notes, Personal Log, year plus 1586

I guided Sheeray to convince the King to build an outpost near the highland foothills. My other Greenlings have contacted a group of bandits. The bandits are exceptionally lazy. It is near impossible to get them to do anything unless they face starvation of death. They love to drink a brew called shittha. They drink it all day. I believe this is the key to my plan.

I have provided copious amounts of shittha. The bandits are in poor health as a result. They are mentally unfit. Yet this is the best state to motivate them without opposition. I risked sending Sheeray to them. He is the only Greenling who can use the quadbeam emitter.

I ordered him to beam them all and command their minds. He instructed them that the guards at the outposts are warlocks. That the guards plan to murder the bandits and eat them. And the outpost has an immense golden treasure under the floorboards. Lastly, that this night is the only time the warlocks are weak. They must attack tonight.

Kin, Lab notes, Personal Log, year plus 1586

I observed the entire battle. There was no possibility of the bandits winning against the guards. If Sheeray had not paralyzed each guard with the emitter the plan would have failed. The bandits spent considerable effort trying to find treasure. There was nothing to find. But the destruction emphasized the threat of the attack.

Kin, Lab notes, Personal Log, year plus 1586

Sheeray has finally convince the King to dig a canal. I worry he used the quad-beam emitter too often. I worry that the King will adapt to the beam and rebel against the Greenling. I suspect the King believes the Greenling is a magical creature. The abomination have many such superstitions. The idea of a canal as a defensive line has some merit. But not much.

Sheeray supplied the king with gold on every visit. The King used the gold for laborers to build his palace. When the construction was completed he had a potential work force without a purpose. The digging of a canal was a continued boon to the local economy. The laborers used their pay to build better housing. It also led to an increase in local population and immigration from neighboring cities.

Kin, Lab notes, Personal Log, year plus 1595

The plan was a success up to this point. But the new lake did not penetrate into the layers below. I need to get the cyanide water into the conglomerate strata. An impenetrable strata near the surface causes the lake to overfill. The lake empties down the valley rather than soaking into the deeper strata.

I waited until the lake was at its lowest annual level. It helps that this year had below average precipitation. As the old Sheeray has died, I instructed my new, least lazy Greenlings to spread a rumor near the city of Genera. He is not as good as Sheeray. He met abomination as they traveled lonely roads. He divulged to them that there is treasure surrounding Lowmont lake. A few abomination ventured to dig pits. I understand the abomination lose interest quickly. I was prepared with a plan.

My Greenlings gathered the richest ore samples from the caves. I instructed the Greenlings to sneak into the pits at night. They buried gold crusted rocks just under the loose rock in the bottom of the pit.

I planted nano-particles on the ore samples so I could watch the abomination as they made the discovery. I delighted to watch the faces of the abomination as they found the treasure. Their eyes open wide. They stare as if they doubt their own senses. Then their face opens with surprise. Finally they rejoice. Sometimes I laugh at the sight.

My plan succeeded. Soon the Lowmont lake valley was full of abomination digging pits. I planted enough treasure to keep them engaged. When enough pits were sufficiently deep I ordered the Greenlings to stop planting the golden treasure.

When the rainy season begins the pits will fill. The cyanide rich water will finally seep into the proper strata.

Kin, Lab notes, Personal Log, year plus 1606

I am on the verge of success. The gold is slowly dissolving off the conglomerate. It is collecting at the shale layer. But an ooze of dissolved rock settles too. There is a little gold and a lot of ooze.

There is no way to collect the gold precipitates without technology. Only one natural cave descends deep enough to directly reach the shale layer. I have an ooze of gold rich clay. I can not get to the ooze without digging miles of mines.

I experiment in the lab endlessly. I need a way to get the gold out of the ooze. I need a way to collect the ooze so it can be processed. It needs to be undetectable to the Saurians. Yesterday, in frustration I threw a zerkay scanner. It broke.

Kin, Lab notes, Personal Log, year plus 1609

I have devised a chemical process to separate the gold from the ooze. I cannot transport the processing chemicals to the gold ooze. I cannot transport the ooze to a processing facility. My only option is very small processors which can transport themselves. I am designing a micro machine which can crawl. I have patterned the machine after the scarab beetle. It will crawl into the lime ooze. It holds a micro processing plant in its abdomen. When it is full of gold it will crawl back to the pod.

Kin, Lab notes, Personal Log, year plus 1618

All my fabrication capabilities are devoted to producing the gold bugs. I produce eight-thousand per day. As the first batch began to return I realized I made an oversight in design. They must be disassembled to get the gold out. It is not time effective to open them. I have abandoned the first batch of gold bugs in the ooze. My second model can dump the gold and return to service.

Kin, Lab notes, Personal Log, year plus 1632

I can track the path of each gold bug. I have mapped the slate layer. I believe there is a low point which is particularly rich. I believe it will be time effective to dig a tunnel to that location. If I install a suction pipe I can suction out the liquidy ooze.

My only impediment is motivating the Greenlings. They must do the hard work. They must dig out a tunnel with prybars and carry baskets. I cannot risk the use of cutting charges. The Saurians would detect it and pinpoint the location.

Kin, Lab notes, Personal Log, year plus 1634

The Greenlings prove almost useless. I contemplated paying abomination to do the work. I decided not for two reasons. One the work is too far underground. The air is poor and the temperature is too hot. Second it is too close to the pod. I cannot risk the abomination knowing about the pod.

If I prepare a special dish for the Greenlings I can get them to excavate one carry basket per day. Only about a third will participate. At this rate the gold bugs will recover the necessary amount of gold before the tunnel is excavated. I proceed with the tunnel as a secondary assurance in case the gold bug project falls short.

Kin, Lab notes, Personal Log, year plus 1702

I had not envisioned the enormous bulk of the gold. I cannot fit any more in the pod. I have begun to deposit it in the tunnels outside the pod. I need to prepare it for transportation. I don't know what technology will be used to transport the gold. I press it into bars and the Greenlings stack it wherever space can be found. I need further direction.

To Kin

I am informed that standard cargo transports will be used to transport the gold. I have not been informed when. I have not been informed how the Saurians will be dealt with. Palletize the gold for transport.

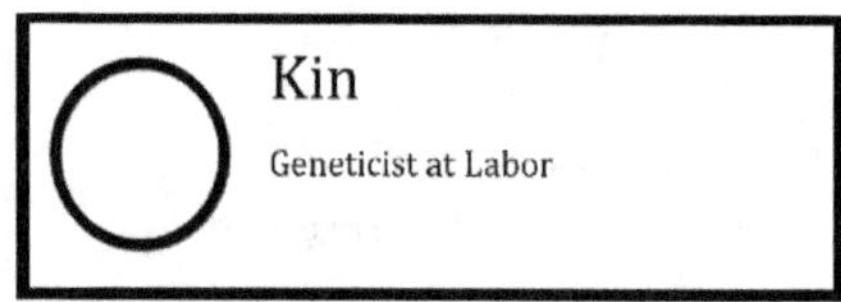

To Baron Rotha

All my fabrication capacity is devoted to gold bug production. I cannot produce pallets unless I cannibalize metal from the pod. I cannot meet schedule without full production of new gold bugs.

I am out of room to store gold, both inside the pod and in the tunnels outside. I need to have it moved to the surface. I have no warehouse. I do not want gold ingots left on the surface for abomination to discover.

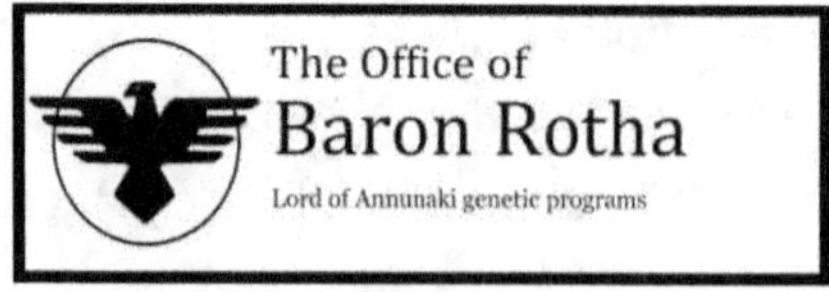

To Kin

Stack the ingots on the surface. Disguise them. I will inform military command that the gold will not be palatized. I will put it on them to devise a method to load the gold.

To Baron Rotha

My Greenlings were never designed to labor. They are too lazy. I have asked too much of my Igigi already. They collect gold pellets and press it into bricks. I deem they will rebel if I ask them to carry heavy loads to the surface. I cannot risk creating an elevator to hoist the gold. I am out of options.

The gold bugs bring three tons of gold every Earth day. I am out of room to store the gold. I am out of options to carry the gold to the surface. As you are aware, we are behind schedule. We race against the rising sun.

To Kin

I congratulate you on your tremendous success. No one had any right to expect that this project could have accomplished so much. We are at the doorway to victory. We will not fail at the last moment. We have no choice but to use the abomination. Devise a plan to employ the abomination - discretely.

Kin, Lab notes, Personal Log, year plus 1704

I contemplate the requirements of employing the abomination. I don't like the conclusion. I cannot let the abomination spread rumors of the existence of so much gold. I will need to destroy the abomination after they complete the task. I will need to keep them captive while they work.

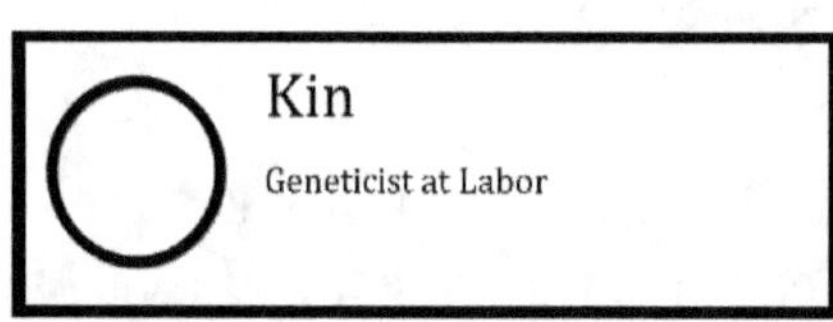

To Baron Rotha

The abomination are intelligent enough to require a reason for their labor. I propose to employ abomination thus: they will carve more suitable tunnels. They will build steps from the surface to the pod. They will carry gold ingots to the surface.

They will use the gold ingots as bricks to construct buildings. They will make a city of gold. The transports must palletize and load the gold.

The city is remote enough it will not draw attention from the abomination or Saurians unless they come close enough to realize the bricks are made of gold.

The first task will be to build city walls to keep the abomination inside. I will destroy the abomination workers after their task is complete. I will require further resources to feed and clothe the abomination. My fabrication facilities are fully employed. My food production resources are insufficient.

To Kin

Your plan is approved. I will secure the additional resources you require. How will you capture the abomination work force?

To Baron Rotha

I will cave in the local mine at Genera and the neighboring city. I will do it at night so the abomination will not be killed. The abomination miners will be unemployed. My Greenlings will entice them with an up-front gold payment to support their families. The Greenlings will entice them with promises of kingly wealth.

To Kin

It is determined that enough gold has been stacked on the surface. Your city of gold project is complete and successful. It will not be necessary for your Igigi to terminate the abomination workers.
Withdraw all resources inside the pod. Transports are scheduled to arrive. They will slaughter any living thing within the walls of the city of gold.

To Kin

I have news of the military gold transportation operation. For the most part it was a success. Eighty percent of transports survived. Our diversion on Mars was mostly successful. Most of the Saurian fighting craft dispatched to the diversion. However a remnant force detected our transports. Our sensory blocking technology was not fully effective. Twenty percent of transports were shot down. They fell back into the atmosphere. They burned up in freefall. I expect they rained globs of molten gold on the surface.

I will relay relevant details as they become available.

To Baron Rotha

May I know the diversion used on mars?

To Kin

A large number of nuclear devices were detonated on the surface. On device detonated every hour for a full Earth day.

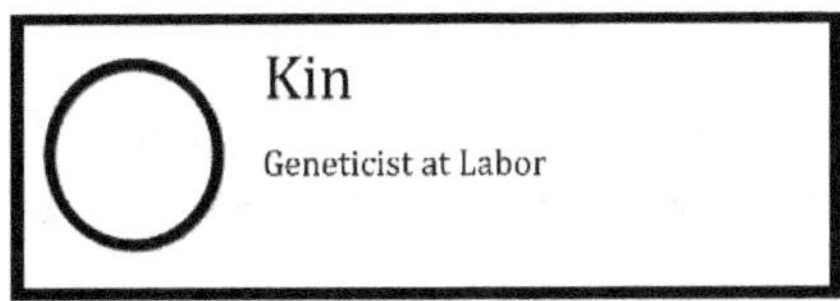

To Baron Rotha

I expect military command understood the blasts would send a detectable sub-plasma tremor across half the galaxy.

To Kin

The blasts were vectored and contained to minimize detection in every direction except toward the galaxy center. This bold move demonstrates the urgency of our project.

The Saurians are at least partially aware of our operation. We have been ordered to hold position. Standby for further orders.

To Kin

This is a summary of the latest project progress statistics.

This nova has proceeded mildly by any measure. The solar system's heliosphere has only charged to 45% saturation. The heliosphere has only reached 36% luminescence. The heliopause has only expanded by 13%. It has not expanded enough to disrupt significant Kuiper belt objects. The terrestrial planets have not hopped from their track. There has not been any substantial electrical discharge between planetary bodies.

There has been speculation about the possibility of plasma twist spikes. Our most distant satellites now confirm the presence of an increased twist in the inflowing Birkeland Current. This transient is certain to produce at least one PT Spike. The spike is predicted to be great in intensity and short in duration. It will affect the sun's magnetic field much more than its solar output. The magnetic burst is predicted to have a strong effect on the poles of the terrestrial planets. The spike is predicted to have a strong effect on the rotation and orientation of the Earth. It is predicted to profoundly upset the oceans of the Earth. It is estimated that more than 80% of life on land will be drowned. It is expected that the areas inhabited by the abomination will be deluged.

To Baron Rotha

By Royal Decree, the abomination are to be terminated. Their use is ended. Their lineage is to be ended. They are to expire in the expected deluge. No living remnant of the abomination shall be retained. No morphogenetic fluids of the abomination shall be retained. The means to reconstitute the abomination shall not be retained. Their existence is to be ended in the flood.

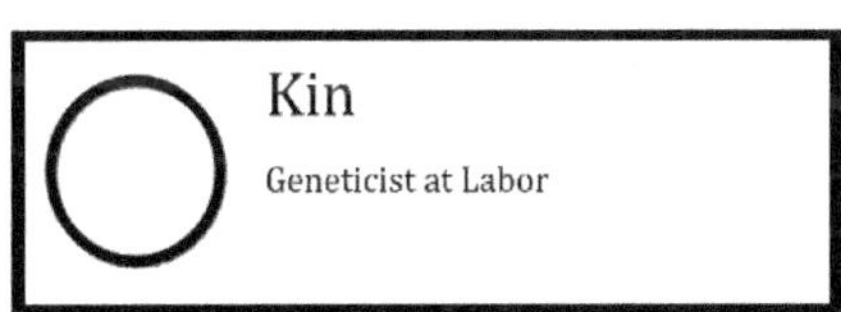

To Baron Rotha

I believe the deluge is not likely to terminate all the abomination. Some of them live in mountains which are unlikely to be deluged. The Saurians took some of them as workers. It is likely that the Saurians maintain some of them in underground facilities. The Saurians should not be the only keeper and ally of the abomination. The King's order denies us the abomination but it does not deny them natural survival. It does not deny the Saurians access.

To Kin

(Reserved for your eyes only)

The abomination have been a controversy from the very start. The Royal family is eager to put this project behind. We will be recognized for our success. The existence of the created worker being is to be minimized. In any public presentation you are to minimize discussion of the use of Anunnaki genetics. We do not deny the abomination. But we do minimize discussion.

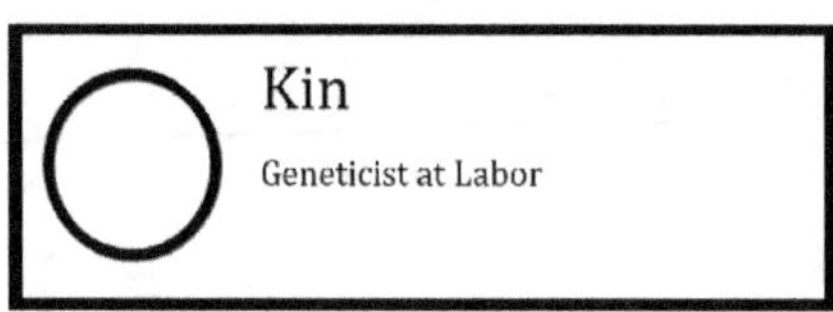

To Baron Rotha

Have we spent so much effort for nothing. Are we to lose it all for political appearances? The creation of a successful worker being is a prize. How can we let it be swept under the carpet. Moreover, how can we give the exclusive use of the abomination to the Saurians?

To Kin

Complete the Royal Decree to the letter.

Kin, Lab notes, Personal Log, year plus 1729

As a side project I have analyzed the distribution of the abomination settlements. I have also predicted possible flood paths. My conclusion is that there is no safe place for the abomination. They risk extinction on the surface.

Kin, Lab notes, Personal Log, year plus 1731

I have completed analysis of all abomination settlements in light of their traditions and customs. I have graded them on aggressiveness, oppressiveness and reasonableness. I find all settlements fit within one of three categories.

Most settlements are large and oppressive cities ruled by aggressive and heartless leaders. Nearly all the remaining settlements are small and lazy towns. The lazy towns have little hope for a greater future. They are places where time moves slowly. Anyone with any ambition moves to the cities.

The third category are small cities with peculiar philosophies. Distinct and peculiar philosophies dominate the local politics. Most of the philosophies are irrational or tyrannical.

Some communities are against all technology. Some have strange and historical traditions. Some have bloody and horrific traditions. Most have a local prophet who purportedly received wisdoms from a god.

I have found one exception. The town of Noaz stands alone as a beacon of hope. They have a reasonable philosophy and rightful conduct. I would have a different opinion of the abomination if they all behaved as the Noaz. I have taken a special interest in them. It would be a pity to see them extinct in the flood.

I have not violated any official decree. I would assume my logs are scrutinized. All my logs, both personal and lab notes, are posted on the Royal Network. If anyone objects to the following plan please let it be known. I plan to send Pixzye to communicate with the Noaz. I intend to inform them of the approaching deluge.

Kin, Lab notes, Personal Log, year plus 1732

One year has passed since I called for a review of my plans. I admit it is unusual to call for comment on my lab notes. But I assume they have been read. I have not received any objection to my plan, so I proceed.

Kin, Lab notes, Personal Log, year plus 1733

My Pixzye emissary inform me the Noaz understand and intend to prepare for the deluge. The Noaz planned to build many boats to float above the flood. I have difficulty explaining the nature of the deluge. Especially through the intermediary of the Pixzye.

The abomination do not have a realistic understanding of the Earth. How could I explain that the oceans would leave their basins and wash over the land with an unimaginable wave of destruction. The Noaz do not even have a conception of a tsunami.

I gave them a design which could surf above such a wave. The design is necessarily disc shaped and fully enclosed. This is the only shape which is both sufficiently strong and able to surf above the wave. I believe they can construct them from local timbers.

Kin, Lab notes, Personal Log, year plus 1738

The Noaz have become zealously devoted to the floating disc project. They have begun construction on several semi-enclosed boats. I have surveilled their progress. They have not understood the nature of the deluge. They will need to survive on the discs for months. They will also need to replant and repopulate afterward. I have instructed them to build bigger vessels and furnish them with food, animals and agricultural seed.

Kin, Lab notes, Personal Log, year plus 1740

The Pixzye argue with the Noaz on every visit. The Pixzye are not able to convey the nature of the catastrophe. The Noaz think they are sailing away on a vacation. They cannot comprehend the extent to which natural ecosystems will be decimated. My conclusion is desperate. Most of the craft will not survive. Maybe none of them will survive.

I have only one clan which is willing to build the water-craft exactly as designed. I have given their chief a clear and detailed plan. He is to build a very large disc craft. I am placing all my hope in his clan. The others will be scattered to their fate.

Kin, Lab notes, Personal Log, year plus 1748

The sun is beginning to twist spike. It is as severe as the worst predictions. The Earth will flip any day. I have recalled all my Greenlings and Pixzye to the pod. We are prepared.

I will lose most, if not all, of my surveillance capabilities. The flood will scatter and bury them. I will attempt to regain a view of the surface as soon as possible. Until then I will not know if any abomination survive.

To Baron Rotha

CC: Associates

Congratulations are due. It has been decreed that the danger of the nova has passed. Solar output continues to decline. Our most distant probe detects a continuing normalization of inflow current. Your project succeeded in producing eighty percent of the ordered gold. Suspended mono-atomic particles reduced nominal radiation by seventy percent. Excess T-radiation was decreased by eighty-three percent. Damage to our planet was minimal. Disruption to our people was negligible. The plan was fully successful.

Lord Rotha is under consideration for commendation and promotion. All your team is commended. The King declares the project victorious.

There are only a few technical questions to be addressed. Afterward you are to be returned victorious to our planet and granted cyber-sleep.

Kin, Lab notes, Personal Log, year plus 1751

She has not flown in a year. Nor has she smiled in my face. I do not know the cause of her lack of joy. I have a feeling that something has been lost that should not be lost. I have a feeling like an empty stomach that I know will never be full again. I do not know what I can do to bring back her joy. It was the warmest in all the history of my heart.

Kin, Lab notes, Personal Log, year plus 1806

The Earth has recovered enough to release the Greenlings and Pixzye to the surface. Digging out of the tunnels proved to be a great task. A great overburden of sediment covers everywhere.

Because food production is limited supplies have been rationed. Most of the Greenlings and half of the Pixzye have left the pod.

Kin, Lab notes, Personal Log, year plus 1807

I surveilled her. I theorized that she might only be without joy in my presence. She was without joy at most times. She took some pleasure in the company of her people. But most of her time was alone and somber.

I watched her in the company of her friend. Her friend had recently reproduced. Airly showed joy when she held the young Pixzye. I think this is the key to her lack of joy. She is at an age ripe for reproduction. I wish to return her to her former happy state.

Kin, Lab notes, Personal Log, year plus 1808

My studies had predicted a thirteen percent chance of a successful inter-species breeding. Reproductive compatibility depended on over forty variable factors. It would have been impossible without the intervention of technology.

It was an improbable but happy fate that the breeding was successful. She carries our offspring. She has radiated a new type of warmth. Perhaps it is indigenous to her species in pregnancy. I have not noted it previously. I continue to monitor her health and that of the fetus.

Kin, Lab notes, Personal Log, year plus 1808

The birth was successful. The old joy I expected to rekindle has been replaced by something new, something warmer and more alive. I see the new baby. There is something in its eyes I have never seen before.

To Baron Rotha

CC: Associates

We reestablished observation of the Earth as soon as possible. Our primary investigation was ecological. Our researchers were exceptionally surprised to discover that seven communities of abomination survived. Seven communities were discovered on three continents. No one can offer a hypothesis of how they survived.

After increased surveillance technology was in operation it detected a large water ship near the largest community. Further investigation confirmed that the abomination had built water ships preemptively. The water ships were of a specialized and previously unknown design.

The Royal Family has opened a formal investigation. You are ordered to participate in this investigation. It has been suggested that someone among the Anunnaki has violated the Royal Decree.

To Dutchess Shera

I shudder to think that anyone among us would violate a Royal Decree. I suspect that the Saurians saved the abomination. I reason that they certainly knew of the solar twist spike. They were known to have both a relationship and interest in the abomination.

To Kin

There is some suspicion that one among the Anunnaki have violated the Royal Decree concerning the extinction of the abomination. Whereas the punishment for such a violation is death, I cannot imagine such is the case. Be vigilant. We have been called to participate in the royal investigation. If you learn of any relevant clue, report it to me directly.

I have lodged my belief that the Saurians are responsible. Nevertheless, we must be vigilant to the investigation.

To Baron Rotha

CC: Associates

You are to be returned to Saturn as heroes and re-inducted into cyber-sleep. The investigation into the survival of the abomination delays your return. A conclusive resolution to the investigation will hasten your victorious return. Be vigilant in your research.

To Kin

Circumstance has compelled me to review recent lab notes. What does it mean that "expenditure of food supplies are at maximum capacity due to consumption by lab denizens"?

To Baron Rotha

Supplies were initially calculated based on a much shorter timeframe. My work has extended beyond all expectations. Pay the details little attention. It is only a technical report.

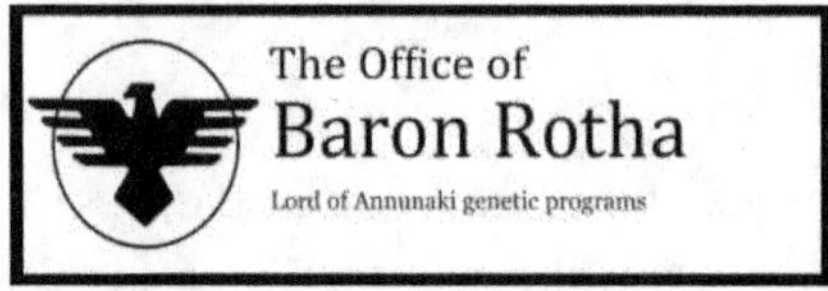

To Kin

Have food expenditures risen? Is the abomination project not ended?

To Baron Rotha

It is only a technical detail I am obligated to include in my report. All expenditures are at acceptable levels. Food levels are fully sufficient.

To Dutchess Shera

(Reserved for your eyes only)

I must inform you before the reports ascend to your level. I have inspected the lab personally. Kin has created many new types of abomination. He has gone far beyond his mandate. He has gone far beyond and contrary to my orders. I was deceived. He has been creating in secret. He has made a menagerie of creatures. He has created like a mad god. There is no sense to be made of the variety of abominations he has created.

I even investigated the stasis tanks. They are full of creatures he had created and put in storage. He has created one-eyed giants, creatures part horse and part abomination, common beast of burden with strange horns, abominations with eight arms.

His secret world is an offence to all reason. I cannot shield him from law or consequence. I warn you, what he has created is beyond any imagination.

I have ordered him to cease all work and remain in the lab.

Kin, Lab notes, Personal Log, year plus 1811

Security alarms indicate an intrusion. Security has never detected any disturbance before. My initial check indicates no malfunctions in the security system. The main hatch cameras are not working. Now the main entry hall cameras are offline. The lab main hatch cameras have just failed. I am sending an alert message to Lord Ratha.

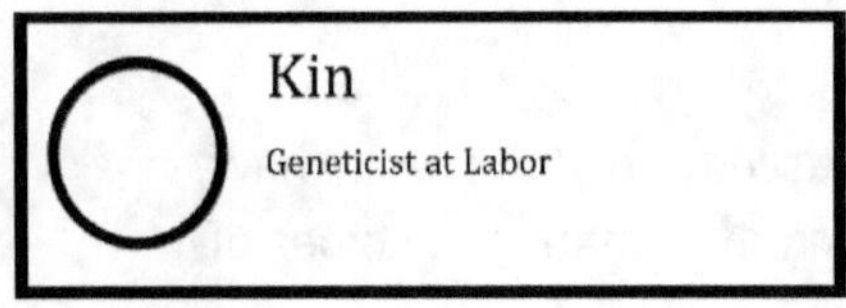

To Baron Rotha

Urgent Report!

The main lab hatch has just been breached. I am attempting to ascertain the identity of the intruders as I write. I see them. The intruders appear to be our Royal Guard. They are approaching me.

To Dutchess Shera and Baron Rotha

I have been accused of the treasonous keeping of secrets. I have made no secret of my ideas, understandings or activities. I have submitted my personal log along with my lab notes.

But I did suspect that no one was analyzing any of my notes. My personal log is part of a very large record. The documents I produce are too voluminous to casually review. I would expect that everything I did was surveilled. But I have seen a pattern. Most of the apparently unimportant information is ignored. Submitting my notes made them effectively secret because no one was watching. But it can not be said that I kept secrets.

To Baron Rotha

(Reserved for your eyes only)

Kin's judgement is before the King. His fate will soon be decided. The King was heard to say, "This common Kin wielded more power than a king, and wrongly."

To Kin

Your judgement is before the King. I have no voice in the matter.

I am shocked to my core. I wonder if you considered how your actions would reflect on me. It is an embarrassment to my family. It is an embarrassment to all Anunnaki. Nevertheless, I hold no ill will toward you.

To Baron Rotha and Dutchess Shera.

I know that judgement is at hand. Here at the end, it is not that I ponder, but rather that I see. It is a mad world. It is a terrible world. I have participated in it. I have even created in it. I could curse the Origin mind. I could curse the All-man. But it changes nothing. I have only one thing left in the world.

I know I am condemned. I know I am guilty. I am numb to the consequences. I have only one concern left in the world.

I don't know what words I could use to convince you. I don't know what argument would light your heart. I don't know, so I'll just say.

Please don't destroy my love. Please let Airly live. I'll go to destruction. I will accept my end without argument. Just let her live.

And if for any reason you are touched, please let her people, the Pixzye, live.

This is my only plea.

To Kin

I return to Saturn. I return to the sweet worlds of cyber-sleep. I bring my deeds with me. I return a victorious hero.

I have been ordered to return. The King himself orders me. The king has given the order. Your life is to be spared in recognition of your service and success. The laboratory will be destroyed. Only the functions of the pod necessary for your survival will remain. Your creations are to remain and live with you.

Escape is denied you. Communication is denied you. Cyber-sleep is denied you. You are condemned to live out your remaining days awake, on Earth and in the pod.

I understand all that has transpired but I cannot comprehend it.

This is my last message to you. My eyes fill with tears. You could have returned with me, a hero. Goodbye.

Epilogue

The mega pod was sealed. Saurian surveillance capabilities could not penetrate the Pod. Kin and Airly both watched as the main hatch locked closed. Kin embraced his love as the Saurians received their last observations.

The Anunnaki have very long lives, even out of cyber-sleep. The Saurians expect Kin still lives. They expect his remaining surveillance network is active. They expect he watches the Earth from his prison.

Now we have heard the tale of our origin. Now we have a view of the ruthless politics between species. Now we understand other species have very different ethics. Now we can receive a warning.

The galaxy is a competitive environment. We are far from alone.

Other species have different natures. They have different morals. They come from different traditions. Do not expect others to be good or benevolent by human standards. Do not equate technology with goodness.

Every species takes advantage where they can. Every species must eat. Every species requires resources. Space travel is very resource intensive. Very few species travel the space-ways without an expectation of profit.

Sentient beings have the capacity to deceive and be deceived. Do not assume a technological species is realistic in their understanding. Do not expect them to have a clear or true worldview. Do not expect them to have a realistic understanding of themselves. They may be highly trained and manipulated in their thinking.

New arrivals are on the Earth now. If we are unwise they will dominate us. They will make us a client state. They will own us. They will take every advantage – unless we are wise - unless we fight.